The
SECRET
of the
TREASURE
KEEPERS

A. M. HOWELL

USBORNE

Contents

CHAPTER 1	TELEPHONE CALL	9
CHAPTER 2	MR KNIGHT	17
CHAPTER 3	MURAL	25
CHAPTER 4	THE PLAN	31
CHAPTER 5	ROOK FARM	37
CHAPTER 6	NOT WELCOME	49
CHAPTER 7	WHISPERS	56
CHAPTER 8	PIPERATORIUM	64
CHAPTER 9	EXCAVATION	74
CHAPTER 10	SECRET	85
CHAPTER 11	KNOCK AT THE DOOR	94
CHAPTER 12	FINAL WARNING	105
CHAPTER 13	MORE TO LEARN	111
CHAPTER 14	EEL MAN	115
CHAPTER 15	BAD TO WORSE	124
CHAPTER 16	BACK TO LONDON	132
CHAPTER 17	OLD THINGS	138
CHAPTER 18	THICKET	144
CHAPTER 19	MR HARTEST	153
CHAPTER 20	EMMA	162
CHAPTER 21	WATCHED	169

Chapter 22	Gone	178
Chapter 23	My Fault	183
Chapter 24	Telegram	190
Chapter 25	The Hut	195
Chapter 26	Birds	200
Chapter 27	Bus	210
Chapter 28	Belvoir Street	218
Chapter 29	Sally	229
Chapter 30	Mr Bond's Buses	239
Chapter 31	Suspicion	249
Chapter 32	The Van	254
Chapter 33	This is the Spot	261
Chapter 34	Blizzard	272
Chapter 35	Proof	281
Chapter 36	Accusations	288
Chapter 37	The Truth	292
Chapter 38	Apologies	303
Chapter 39	Change	310
Chapter 40	Six Months Later	316

Author's Note

Usborne Quicklinks

Acknowledgements

Further Titles from A.M. Howell

ROOK
FIELD

MAGPIE
FIELD

EEL MAN'S
HUT

GULL
FIELD

EEL
FIELD

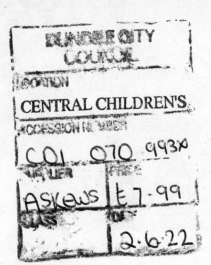

CHAPTER I

Telephone Call

Ruth leaned against the wall in the depths of the British Museum, as the telephone continued to ring. She shifted position, her scuffed brown shoes squeaking on the linoleum floor. The telephone in the nearby office demanded attention, but it was late Monday afternoon and most museum staff had already shrugged on woollen coats and scarfs and headed into the February gloom to spend time with their families over the school holidays. Ruth's eyes settled on the office where the ringing was coming from, and the small nameplate attached to the half-open door.

Mr S. Knight

Curator of British Collections

Except Mr Knight wasn't just in charge of British Collections, he was also the person Ruth's mum, Harriett Goodspeed, museum volunteer and aspiring archaeologist, was being interviewed by in the coins room along the hall in the hope of getting a paid job. Ruth chewed on her bottom lip and glanced at the office next door to Mr Knight's. The man who worked in there had left ten minutes ago and she had seen no one else since. He had flashed Ruth a quick smile, which was also laced with a dollop of sympathy. "I hope your mum gets the museum assistant job. I'm afraid Mr Knight's in a sore mood. He's still smarting from not having found anything of interest at the Sussex dig," he'd said, adjusting the angle of his black hat.

Ruth had wished the man a pleasant evening, though her shoulders had drooped a little at learning of Mr Knight's poor mood. While her mum was in awe of Mr Knight and his encyclopaedic knowledge of British archaeology, Ruth didn't warm to the near-permanent downward curl of his lip and his ability to look through her as if she was swathed in a mist of invisibility. But despite her own thoughts on Mr Knight, this interview was very important and had preoccupied her mum for weeks. While the wireless hummed in the background and Ruth searched through their well-thumbed cookery books for recipes that would not use up all their precious post-war egg and sugar rations, her mum had diligently pored over her books and field notes late into the evenings to ensure she was fully prepared for today's interview.

Ruth shifted from one foot to the other as the telephone continued to ring. Its shrill tone swallowed up the corridor's calm silence and was terribly annoying. Whoever was on the other end of the line was persistent. Puffing out a breath and walking the few steps to Mr Knight's office, Ruth pushed the door fully open. The room was large, with tall rectangular windows reflecting the inky blackness outside. An anglepoise lamp on the desk threw a spot of light onto leather-bound books and cardboard folders filled with handwritten notes. Floor to ceiling shelves bore the weight of files, each with a small, typed label pasted on the spine. *Roman Hoards; Fourth Century. Viking Silver; Tenth Century.* The office smelled musty and old, in keeping with the ancient dates on the folders.

Balanced on the edge of Mr Knight's desk was the ringing telephone. Ruth's throat constricted as she saw it was vibrating so forcefully that it was likely to dive to the floor any second, quite possibly taking some of Mr Knight's books and folders with it. Rushing into the room, she placed both hands on the telephone, anchoring it to the desk. Making a quick decision she picked up the receiver. She straightened her neck and took a deep breath. "Um…hello. British Museum here. Mr Knight's office."

"Oh. Hello. Someone is there after all," replied a woman. She sounded crackly and very far away and Ruth pressed the receiver hard to her ear. "I was about to ring off, but it's raining here and I made a special trip to the telephone box," continued the woman.

Beneath the crackles of the poor line, Ruth could hear that the woman had a warm voice, the exact opposite of the shrill ring still echoing in her ears. "Yes, the weather is beastly, isn't it?" she replied, relaxing a little.

The woman coughed and there was a short pause on the other end of the line while she gathered her breath. "Yes. Beastly is a good word for it. Particularly here in the Cambridgeshire Fens," she croaked. "Right. Well.

I was calling to see if Mr Knight had read my letter."

Ruth chewed on her bottom lip, realizing that she hadn't thought this through. She had been so intent on stopping the telephone from ringing she hadn't considered that the person on the end of the line might want to ask her a question. "Your letter," repeated Ruth with a frown, casting her eyes around the chaotic room and the jumble of papers, files and books.

"I sent it two weeks ago. It's really quite urgent," said the woman. There was another pause. Ruth could hear the steady thrum of rain against the telephone box the woman was calling from. "I've been watching for the post every day but got no reply. I wonder if the letter is lost?"

Ruth detected a wheeze in the woman's voice. The sound of the rain intensified, and she felt a bolt of sympathy. She cast her eyes around the office again. There didn't seem to be a tray for correspondence, or anything resembling a filing system at all. Perhaps Mr Knight saw his office as having some sort of order, just as she did with the casually dropped clothes on her bedroom floor. But the room seemed to be in a proper state of chaos and she did not know where to begin searching for this woman's letter. "I'm afraid I don't know anything about a letter. Perhaps you could call back tomorrow and speak to Mr Knight then?" Ruth asked hopefully.

"I went to the post office in Ely and paid the correct postage," said the woman, ignoring Ruth's suggestion. "Are you Mr Knight's secretary? Perhaps you could take a message?"

Ruth glanced to the corridor, straining to hear the squeak of shoes, feeling more than a little worried now about being caught in Mr Knight's office. Thankfully it was still quiet. "Yes, I can take a message," she said, quickly reaching for a pencil and a scrap of discarded paper.

"If you can tell Mr Knight that some of the treasure – well, what I hope is treasure – is still in the field. The ground is becoming waterlogged, and snow is forecast this week," said the woman. "I just don't know what to do for the best. Do I take it out, or leave it where it is? I'm worried it will get damaged."

Ruth drew in a long breath and watched the tiny dust motes dance under the gleam of Mr Knight's desk lamp. "Treasure," she repeated, carefully printing the word on the scrap of paper.

"Can you tell Mr Knight that I'm keen to establish if

the items are worth something. I remembered his name from the wireless – when he was interviewed about some Roman silver found a few years back. A similar treasure trove might well save my farm." The woman had a sudden coughing fit.

Ruth winced and held the receiver away from her ear until the woman had gathered her breath again.

"Sorry, I just can't seem to shake off this darned cold. You *will* pass the message to Mr Knight, won't you?" insisted the woman, whose voice was tight with the effort of withholding further coughs.

"Yes. Of course," said Ruth, staring at her hastily scribbled notes.

"Mr Knight can reach me at Rook Farm. We're just south of Ely. I'm afraid I don't have a telephone, so he'll need to write or send a telegram."

"Don't worry, I will pass the message on. Oh. I didn't take down your name…"

"Mrs Sterne. My name is Mrs Mary Sterne," the woman wheezed. "Goodbye then."

"Goodbye, Mrs Sterne," replied Ruth. There was a click as Mrs Sterne ended the call. Ruth returned Mr Knight's telephone receiver and looked again at the piece of paper in her hand.

Treasure.

Waterlogged and damaged.

Value?

Save my farm.

Rook Farm – south of Ely.

Mrs Mary Sterne.

There was the bump of a door closing along the corridor and voices. *Mum and Mr Knight.* Quickly folding the paper, Ruth slipped out of the office and took up her previous position of leaning against the wall. Her heart was beating a little faster than usual. She thought of the museum's silver coins and plates she had watched her mum unpack after they'd been stored away during the war. As items were put back on display, Ruth would catch a glimpse of the excitement archaeologists must have felt when discovering these finds. She felt a growing sense of excitement herself now as she wondered exactly what treasure Mrs Sterne had discovered at Rook Farm.

CHAPTER 2

Mr Knight

R uth clutched Mrs Sterne's telephone message as Mr Knight's shoes squeaked along the corridor towards his office. The heels of her mum's shoes clicked as she hurried two steps behind. Despite her mum's best efforts to make herself presentable for the interview, a blue ink spot bled into the cuff of her fawn-brown jumper and her bobbed hair stood on end as if she had received a mild electric shock. Ruth adjusted her headband and tucked her own blonde hair behind her ears, feeling the same frizz that plagued them both.

Mr Knight's forehead was creased, and his lips were pressed together.

Ruth let out a small breath of dismay. Had it not gone well? Perhaps now was not the right time to pass on the message.

In any event Mr Knight ignored Ruth and entered his office, while Ruth's mum paused outside and raised her eyebrows.

"What happened?" mouthed Ruth silently.

"Mrs Goodspeed?" Mr Knight called in an irritated tone.

Ruth's mum gave a small shake of her head, pushed her shoulders back and entered the office, pulling the door almost closed behind her.

Putting the telephone message in her coat pocket, Ruth could not stop herself from creeping to the door and listening quietly.

"I am sorry, Mrs Goodspeed. While you correctly identified all but two of the coins I asked you to examine a moment ago, I feel you need more practical experience before I can consider you for a paid job at the museum. Gain some more work experience on archaeological digs and we'll talk again." Mr Knight's voice was like that of a teacher telling off a pupil for having made a mistake in their spelling test.

Ruth winced, thinking back to the harsh words she had received from Mr Knight while accompanying her mum on an archaeological dig in Kent the previous summer. Ruth had been excited to escape the heat, which pulsed through London's pavements. But what she hadn't anticipated was that she'd be consumed with the aura of excitement and anticipation that hung over everyone who worked on the dig at the thought of finding something old and untouched for centuries. Ruth had found it contagious and soon asked her mum if she might have a try at excavating, using a spare trowel, herself. Her mum had readily agreed, and Ruth remembered keenly the smell of the sun-baked earth, the feel of the slim wooden-handled trowel and the sound of it scraping carefully across the soil as she mirrored her mum's movements. Her eyes had been wide and alert for something ancient and valuable, but then the sudden low voice of Mr Knight in her ear demanded she stop immediately. "Children are clumsy and make mistakes. Put that tool down at once," he'd growled.

Ruth had felt a sharp stab of humiliation as the eyes of archaeologists and other volunteers threw her pitying glances. Her mother had tried to appease Mr Knight as Ruth squirmed, telling him she may be a child, but she was observant, a quick learner and would be supervised carefully. But Mr Knight had dismissed them both with a wave of a hand, his attention focused on the young man Ruth had been working next to. He had just uncovered what appeared to be a coin. It had caused a small crowd to gather round and clap him on the back, saying things like, "Well done!" and "What a find, old chum", but the immediate excitement Ruth felt had been dampened by Mr Knight's attitude.

Hearing her mum clear her throat inside Mr Knight's office now, Ruth pushed the unhappy memory away and turned her attention back to the conversation.

"You supervised the work I undertook on the dig last summer. You said my attention to detail was good. I do believe I am qualified for this position," her mum was saying.

"Mrs Goodspeed, my decision is final," said Mr Knight curtly. "There is a fine line between persistence and insolence, and I fear you are heading for the latter. You need to remember your position here. While you have clearly read many books on archaeology, you have no university degree and no formal qualifications.

Archaeology is about gaining experience as much as anything else. Now I must draw this meeting to a close as I've a train to catch to the Sussex dig. I'll see you back here at the museum nine o'clock sharp, Thursday morning, to continue cataloguing the coins."

Ruth felt a swell of sympathy for her mum and a fresh burst of dislike for Mr Knight.

There was a short silence. "Well…thank you for taking the time to interview me," replied her mother in a thin voice.

The meeting was ending. Ruth quickly walked away from the office door.

Her mother emerged, closing the door behind her. She blew out a long breath.

"It didn't go well then," said Ruth in a small voice.

"I might have a passion for archaeology, but I have no qualifications and don't yet have the experience of many people who work here," her mum said, with a dismal sigh, shrugging on her grey coat.

"Do we really need the money from this job that badly?" asked Ruth quietly.

"I'm afraid so," her mum replied with a grimace. "I need a proper career to pay the rent and I'm determined to do something I enjoy."

An onion-sized lump rose in Ruth's throat as she thought about why the job at the museum, and the money it would bring, was so important.

"Come on," Ruth's mum said, winding her knitted scarf round her neck. "We still have an egg and the remainder of Friday's loaf, which we can toast in the grill. We'll walk down Oxford Street and through Hyde Park; it will save the tube fare."

Ruth gave her mum a weak smile and pulled on her bottle-green woollen hat and gloves. As they walked along the museum corridor and away from Mr Knight's office, she remembered with a jolt the message about the treasure at Rook Farm. She paused and looked back. She could almost sense Mr Knight's displeasure at the interview with her mum curling under the crack in his door, like the thick smog that plagued London this winter. She imagined his displeasure deepening at the discovery that a twelve-year-old girl had been in his office without permission (particularly one he thought prone to clumsiness and making mistakes). But he needed to know what Mrs Sterne had said about her treasure find.

Seeing that that her mum was chatting to the security guard at the key pound, where all museum staff handed in their office keys at the end of each working day, Ruth pulled the message from her pocket and ran back towards Mr Knight's office. As she neared his door it opened and Mr Knight stepped out, wearing a thick brown winter overcoat that made him look formidable in a bear-like way. His dark eyes met hers and she ground to a halt.

"Running in the corridors is not permitted," he said, giving Ruth a fearsome glare as he put on his hat.

"Oh...um...sorry...but..." stammered Ruth, holding out the handwritten message. Her fingers trembled.

"I'm late for my train. Where is your mother? Children should not be in this part of the museum unaccompanied," Mr Knight said irritably, not even looking at the note. He made a swivelling gesture with his hand and pointed along the corridor towards the exit.

Heat flashed up the back of Ruth's legs and she let her outstretched arm drop to her side. She hurried back the way she had come, the squeak of Mr Knight's shoes following close behind.

Ruth's mum was still standing by the key pound and looking a little puzzled. "Where did you get to?" she asked, her eyes widening as she looked beyond Ruth to Mr Knight.

"Mrs Goodspeed. The working corridors of the museum are no place for children," said Mr Knight, his voice as taut as a drum.

Ruth pressed her lips together and threw her mum an apologetic look.

"Yes. Of course," her mum replied with a frown.

Giving a sharp nod to the security guard, Mr Knight handed over his key then swept past them like an unpleasant breeze and headed out of the staff door.

"What was that all about?" asked Ruth's mum as they also exited the staff door into the bitter evening air.

Ruth pulled on her woollen hat. Mr Knight hadn't taken the note and she hadn't been bold enough to find the words to tell him about it. But she couldn't keep the message she had taken from Mrs Sterne a secret; it did sound quite urgent. And what if she called again and Mr Knight discovered a message had been taken and not passed on?

"Mum," Ruth said, as they walked side by side down the steps "There's something I need to tell you."

24

CHAPTER 3

Mural

As they walked home along the glistening London streets, Ruth's mum was a little exasperated to learn of the afternoon's events. "You should have passed on the message to Mr Knight straight away, Ruth. It does sound important."

Ruth tightened her grip on her torch. The war might have ended two-and-a-half years ago, in 1945, but the street lights were still patchy. Walking without a torch through the low-hanging and polluted smog could result in clipped heels and bumped shins if you accidentally collided with someone else. "I did try to give it to him, but all he wanted to do was tell me off."

Ruth's mum sighed as they continued on past a yawning hole between buildings, where bomb-blasted rubble was being loaded onto a truck. On the wireless, Ruth had heard that piles of London rubble were being shipped to New York to create new land from the sea. She thought of people's bedroom walls, favourite bookshops and places of work being sunk into water on the other side of the world, so that new lives could be built on top of them.

It was a miracle that the bombs, which rained down on London during the Blitz, had avoided their home – a former coach house that lay just south of Hyde Park. There had been close shaves of course, including one memorable occasion when she and her mum had returned from sheltering in an underground station to find two air raid wardens pushing a huge, unexploded bomb in a wheelbarrow. It had landed directly outside their front door! Ruth suddenly felt a little dizzy at the memory and paused in the street.

"Mr Knight can be difficult," said Ruth's mum, stopping too. Bus wheels hissed and the glow of other people's torches wavered like fireflies as they hurried past. "He isn't always the easiest person to work with.

But I must prove myself to him if I'm to get a job and provide for us both. Let's talk about what to do with Mrs Sterne's message when we get home."

Ruth stared after her mum as she set off again, narrowly avoiding a collision with a man in a dark suit and hat, who was using his torch to read his newspaper as he walked. She had only complicated matters by answering Mr Knight's telephone. An unhappy warmth heated Ruth's cheeks as she adjusted her grip on the torch and hurried on.

Back at home, Ruth switched on a single bar of the electric fire to warm the living room. She laid the dining table for two and listened to her mum preparing tea in the kitchen as the wireless hummed quietly. Usually her mum whistled or sang along to the various tunes, but this evening she was quiet and subdued. It was as if Mr Knight had squashed all of the hope from her and it made Ruth feel slightly unmoored.

Slipping upstairs to her bedroom, Ruth approached the painted mural of the mews where they lived, that stretched across one of her walls. Her dad had been a signpainter before the war and had lovingly created it when she was small. She kneeled before it as she had done so many times in the past, pressing a hand to the replica of their converted coach house. Her tiny painted family of three stood merrily waving in front of the black front door.

Her dad had served in the Navy during the war and each time he returned on shore leave he had found time to add a new small detail to the mural. Mrs Drake's fluffy white cat stalking along a roof (she'd been so worried about the cat being a target during the Blitz, she'd lovingly sewn it a small blackout jacket with buttons). Mr Peters in his patriotic Union flag trousers (which his wife had sewn from real flags). Their neighbour Michael's toy Spitfire hanging from the window of his bedroom. Her dad had finally been released from his post in the Navy the previous summer. But just after Christmas, he and her mum had told Ruth that, while they still rubbed along together well and were great friends, they did not love each other in the same way as they had before the war started and had grown apart. They had decided to divorce. Ruth loved both of her parents dearly and was deeply unhappy at this news, but perhaps also wasn't entirely surprised. Her dad had been away for seven years, apart from his snatched visits of shore leave.

In early January her dad had moved out and only then had it struck Ruth that this was to be a permanent arrangement. Recently her parents had been having lengthy discussions about the practicalities of their amicable divorce while they thought she was upstairs occupied with homework (she was actually sitting at the top of the stairs listening, with her chin resting on her knees). One evening a few weeks earlier she had overheard some particularly disturbing news.

"The rent on my flat means I won't be able to give you as much money each month for household bills and such like. Things are tight while I build up my sign-painting business again, Harriett," her dad had said apologetically.

There had been a short pause.

"What are you saying?" her mum had eventually replied.

"I'm saying we need more money. The rent on this house is expensive. Could you move somewhere smaller and cheaper?" her dad had asked.

Ruth had crept back to her bedroom, her head buzzing. *Move house?* But that was unthinkable. She felt her chest tighten now at their predicament as she examined the mural.

If they moved to a new house, her mural and all of the memories that accompanied it would be left behind too. The wall might even be painted over by the new occupants. She did not think she could bear for her family's past to be obliterated in that way. And what if their new home was further from her dad's flat, meaning she saw him less often? Her throat thickened with tears as she desperately tried to think of a way to stop this from happening.

CHAPTER 4

The Plan

Ruth was still looking at the mural on her wall when her mum called to say that tea was ready. She gave the mural one last lingering look, then traipsed downstairs. She realized she had quite possibly made things worse by answering Mr Knight's telephone. Now he would never consider her mum for a job at the museum if what she had done made him cross. Then there would be no possibility of them staying in the house she loved so much. She chewed on her bottom lip, remembering that her dad said most problems could be solved by having a jolly good think. Ruth thought hard, remembering her conversation with Mrs Sterne. She had been very anxious about the treasure becoming waterlogged or damaged because of the worsening weather. What had she found?

Staring at the tea table, Ruth thought back to the Kent dig. The archaeologists had worked carefully to remove the ancient coins the young man had found, anxious not to cause any damage. It would be dreadful if whatever Mrs Sterne had found became damaged. Mr Knight was away at the Sussex dig until Thursday and no one else knew about this. If he had taken the note from her, immediate action might have been taken and someone from the museum might have been dispatched to Rook Farm to investigate.

As Ruth filled glasses of water from the kitchen tap and carried them to the dining table, the thought of Mr Knight sending someone to Rook Farm skittered inside her head like a marble. An idea began to take shape and form into something bold and bright as her mum brought through the plates of egg on toast and sat down.

Ruth strode to her coat hanging on a hook by the front door and pulled the telephone message from the pocket. "I've an idea of what to do about Mrs Sterne's message," she said, handing her mum the scrap of paper, then sitting at the table and lacing her hands together.

Her mum looked up from cutting her toast into small pieces.

"Mrs Sterne is worried the treasure she's found will get damaged. Mr Knight is away in Sussex and can't help, but you might be able to, Mum," said Ruth.

Ruth's mum shook her head. "I couldn't do anything without Mr Knight's agreement."

Ruth pushed her plate to one side and leaned forward. "During the war you used to say it was important to do what was right, no matter what the consequences. Shouldn't we help Mrs Sterne? Surely Mr Knight would want whatever has been found to be saved. If something does get damaged it could be my fault for not passing on the note. That would be rotten."

Ruth's mum tilted her head to one side. She seemed to be deep in thought. "Did this Mrs Sterne seem very worried on the phone?" she asked eventually.

Ruth nodded, telling her mum the reason Mrs Sterne had contacted Mr Knight was because she had heard him talking on the wireless about the discovery of Roman silver.

A starry glint began to gather in the corners of her mum's eyes. She picked up the telephone message, pushed her chair back and walked to the window, staring out at the view along the cobbles and to the houses nestling either side. Their coach house stood in the far corner of the mews – a courtyard of houses formerly used as stables for the grand Kensington mansions they were built behind. They rarely pulled the curtains closed, eager for glimpses of sky now there were no longer blackouts.

Her mum turned. "It is curious that Mrs Sterne mentioned Roman silver. Could she have found something similar?"

"Could it be coins do you think, like on the Kent dig?" said Ruth.

"Perhaps. The Romans did settle in the East. Ely is near Cambridge. And Rook Farm should be easy enough to find," her mum mused.

"What? You mean we should go there?" asked Ruth in surprise.

Ruth's mum's cheeks flushed as she continued to look at the note. "I could telephone the museum and leave a message for Mr Knight. I could tell him about Mrs Sterne and how we have gone to Rook Farm to see what she's found. We could stay at a bed and breakfast in Ely tomorrow night, then return to London the day after on Wednesday. I'll be volunteering at the museum on Thursday and can tell Mr Knight all about it then."

"*We* can stay in a bed and breakfast?" exclaimed Ruth. "I can come too?"

"If you'd like to," replied her mum, arching an eyebrow.

Ruth grinned and nodded. Her smile dipped. "But do you think Mr Knight will mind us going?" she asked, remembering his down-curled lips after her mum's interview and the telling-off she had received for running in the corridor.

"It might please him. Maybe it will prove that I am worthy of the job at the museum," said her mum, her voice full of renewed optimism.

Ruth was starting to feel optimistic too.

"Staying overnight would cost a bit. It would mean tightening our belts even more when we get home," her mum continued.

"I like our powdered egg rations," said Ruth with a smile.

A laugh burst from her mum's lips. "You really are intent on helping."

Ruth gave a small shrug. She was desperate to know what treasure might be waiting for them, and if their visit to Rook Farm did please Mr Knight, he might change his mind and offer her mum a job, which would be the answer to their problems.

"I'll take my tools just in case there is some excavating to be done. Let me telephone your dad and tell him we'll be away," said her mum.

Ruth felt a buzz of excitement. She thought again of the young man working next to her on the dig last summer. His thrill at finding the coins that had been buried for so many years had been infectious. With no Mr Knight to tell her off, Ruth hoped she could help her mum with any archaeological excavations on the farm. And imagine if she found some treasure herself! What had seemed before as if it would be a grey and dreary school holiday, had taken an unexpected and thrilling turn.

CHAPTER 5

Rook Farm

"**A**re you sure this is Rook Farm?" asked Ruth, clutching their small overnight suitcase as stinging rain buffeted them from all sides. They were standing at the end of a long, muddy track, pools of water gathering in its ruts and dips. At the far end of the track, Ruth could see a huddle of buildings.

"Well, this is where the bus driver told us to get off," said Ruth's mum. The hope that had flushed her face a rosy pink since they'd begun their journey at King's Cross train station faded a little as she adjusted her head scarf.

The journey had been uneventful, the train filled with day trippers and children with parents visiting friends and family for the school holidays. The smell of lemon drops and spam sandwiches filled the warm carriages as people sat close together, chattering and laughing despite the dullness outside.

As their connecting train from Cambridge to Ely headed north, Ruth had pressed her nose to the window and watched the landscape flatten as if being pressed with an iron. Gunmetal-grey clouds whipped across the vast, open fields that stretched as far as the eye could see, interspersed with the occasional thicket of bare-branched trees and ditches flowing high with water.

"We're in the Fens now," her mum had said, looking up from her book on British Archaeology and glancing out of the train window.

"What's a fen?" asked Ruth, as the train chugged through a small and deserted station.

"It's an area of marshland; a coastal plain that runs all the way up to Norfolk and Lincolnshire. It's very low lying and used to be flooded with water. But now much of the area is drained by pumps so the land can be farmed," said her mum.

"It's very bleak," Ruth said, staring at the furrows of

dark-as-midnight soil in the fields. "It's hard to imagine there's anything at all to be found here, apart from mud…and vegetables."

Her mum smiled and looked up from her book again. "There are always things to find. Although it's the setting and landscape that give us the real clues to the past, often more than the objects you'll find buried in the soil."

Ruth nodded, remembering the excited shouts and whoops from the archaeologists and volunteers as they'd gathered round at the Kent dig after the young man had found the coins. A grassy mound in a farmer's field, which her mum had called a barrow, had guided the archaeologists to choose that spot to excavate. It had turned out to be a burial mound. The earth could certainly reveal surprises and she wondered again what Mrs Sterne had found on her land.

"Come on," her mum said now, swinging her rucksack of tools onto her back as the bus that had transported them from Ely rumbled away. Just like the farm track, the road dipped and rose in a peculiar way and its wheels splashed through the endless pools of water.

Her mum's rucksack bumped up and down on her

back with a *whump-whump-whump* as they set off towards the farm. She had packed two trowels, field pegs and twine, a tape measure, field notebook and compass. Her mum said this was the minimum necessary to undertake a basic excavation and Ruth had felt a surge of anticipation at the thought that she may be allowed to help.

It was just after lunch, but darkness already seemed to be chasing them as they pushed through the rain and dodged the puddles and dips.

"I hope we have a chance to see what's what before we head back to find a bed and breakfast in Ely," her mum said staring straight ahead.

Ruth wondered what sort of welcome they would receive. She hoped Mrs Sterne would sit them in front of a crackling fire and serve them crumpets dripping with freshly churned butter and home-made strawberry jam. Friends who had been evacuated to the countryside during the war had told tales of fresh air, vegetables, and meat every single day. This had resulted in them returning half a head taller and with a rosiness in their cheeks that Ruth could never hope to have while living in London. At times she had felt a little envious.

Evacuation had been voluntary but because Ruth

was three, so under school age, when the war began, her mum would have been evacuated with her. But this was something her mum had been wary of agreeing to, having heard that many evacuees were not even told where they would be evacuated to. She had made the decision they would stay in London and wait. When the expected bombing of cities failed to happen during the first year of the war, many evacuees returned to London, their parents deciding the risks were not as great as the government had suggested. But when Ruth was four the Blitz had begun. The deluge of nightly air attacks by the Germans on British industry and cities was imprinted like ink on Ruth's early memories. By that time her mum had a job helping the war effort and there was no question of them leaving London. Like many others, they stayed in the city and waited the war out. Ruth still occasionally wondered what it would have been like to be evacuated – and her mum too. Perhaps this visit to Rook Farm might give them both a taste of the experiences her friends had spoken of.

After fifteen minutes of trudging along the track through the sheeting rain, they arrived at a farm gate. Beyond it stood a small house, its paintwork on the greyish side of white, the slate roof sagging like a pillow at one end. A tangle of ivy clung to the structure like a barnacle on a rock and rain slid from the roof tiles of the small porch above the front door, splattering mud up the walls.

In front of the house lay a large concrete yard surrounded by assorted wooden barns, some seeming close to collapse, as well as a chicken coop where a few bedraggled birds pecked and clucked, and a stable block. A well-tended vegetable plot sat close to the stable and Ruth saw the door to one of the stalls was open. As she stood looking, a boy in a black mackintosh and boots, perhaps a year or so older than her, emerged and dumped a forkful of hay into the wheelbarrow that was standing outside.

"We're in the right place," said Ruth's mum, nodding at the sign on the gate. *Rook Farm.* The black painted letters were faded, very much like their surroundings. It certainly didn't fit with the image in Ruth's head of rosy-faced children playing in the yard, chickens climbing on haystacks and a tangle of flowers climbing over the front door. But then again it was the middle of winter.

As her mum grappled with the gate catch, there was a distant clunking noise in the field closest to the house. Ruth turned and saw a farmer with a cart being pulled by a solid-looking horse. The farmer paused every few steps, bent, then hurled the things he had picked up into the cart. Could that be Mr Sterne? Ruth looked back along the track they had just walked up. The farm was isolated and seemed to have no neighbours. Birds cawed overhead, their black wings bustling in the wind as they swooped across the yard.

"Rooks," said her mum. "My father used to say they brought bad fortune, not that I believed him."

Ruth shivered, feeling a sudden sense of unease as she watched one or two of the birds settling on the roof of the biggest barn.

"Let's go and knock on the front door," said Ruth's mum.

Ruth slipped through the gate and fumbled with the unfamiliar catch. Securing it on her third attempt, she saw the boy was standing by his wheelbarrow now, leaning on his pitchfork. He watched warily as Ruth followed her mum to the farmhouse, anxious to get out of the rain, which was dripping unpleasantly down the neck of her coat.

Standing under the porch, Ruth placed the small suitcase by the front door and waited while her mum knocked. She heard the gruff bark of a dog inside and the door bumped, as if the animal had hurled itself against it. Ruth took a step back out into the yard, as the dog continued to snarl. She had been wary of dogs ever since her dad had allowed her to pet one in the park some years earlier and it had nipped the tips of her fingers.

The door opened and a young woman with raven-black hair, wearing tan-coloured dungarees, peered out. A black-and-white collie dog snapped by her heels; its dark eyes narrowed.

The woman took hold of the dog's collar and gently pulled him back into the house. "Can I help you?" she asked looking at them both with interest.

Ruth stared at the dog. The woman didn't seem to be holding its collar very tightly. It could escape at any moment. She curled her hands into fists.

The woman looked at Ruth and threw her a quick smile. "Don't worry about Dash. He always barks when people come to the house, not that we get many visitors. He's very old and wouldn't hurt a flea."

Ruth's mum stepped forward and held out her hand.

"I'm Mrs Goodspeed, but please call me Harriett. I'm from the British Museum. This is my daughter, Ruth."

"I'm Audrey," said the woman, quickly shaking Ruth's mum's hand. Something darted across Audrey's face, so lightning quick Ruth couldn't quite grasp it. But if she had been asked to guess, she would have said she seemed nervous. "You've come to see Mary about the treasure then?"

"Yes, that's right," said Ruth's mum.

Ruth heard a noise behind her and saw the boy by the stables had sidled closer. He was still holding the pitchfork and looking at them with ill-disguised suspicion. She smiled at him. His shoulders dipped and he looked away. That wasn't very friendly. Ruth clenched her toes, which were tingling with cold inside her shoes.

"Joe, come over here and say hello. These folks have come from London, from the museum," called Audrey.

The boy gave an almost imperceptible shake of his head. He kicked sulkily at a clod of earth in the yard, jamming on his sopping wet cap.

Ruth turned away, wondering why he wasn't being very welcoming.

"Here comes Mary now," said Audrey. "She was out in the fields before dawn."

The farmer who had been in the field with the cart and horse was now striding across the yard towards them. Ruth had thought it was man but could clearly see she had been mistaken. The woman's cap was pulled low, her mackintosh was slick with rain and her boots were splattered with thick mud. Her cheeks were pale and damp and she coughed as she walked, her face twisting with each breath as if she were being pricked with pins.

Ruth's mum strode across the yard, held out her hand and introduced them both.

Mrs Sterne's eyes brightened, then narrowed with confusion. "But I only telephoned the museum yesterday...how did you...?"

Ruth's mum pumped Mrs Sterne's hand up and down enthusiastically. "Yes. I work as a volunteer at the museum. It was my daughter Ruth you spoke to yesterday on the telephone. I was talking to Mr Knight at the time." She paused, her cheeks flushing, as if someone had just dipped a brush into paint and swirled them with a rosy pink.

"Mr Knight sent you then?" asked Mary, looking confused.

Ruth threw an anxious glance at her mum.

"Well, not exactly," said Ruth's mum.

"Mum left him a message to tell him we were coming," chipped in Ruth, feeling it was important to help explain as she had contributed to the problem.

"Your message seemed urgent and as Mr Knight is away on a dig for a few days I felt it important I came straight away," said Ruth's mum.

Mrs Sterne's drawn features seemed to have a renewed glow at their arrival. "I see. Well, thank you for coming to help. I just hope it won't be a wasted journey for you. Come inside out of the rain." She paused, taking a wheezy breath. "You'll have to excuse the state we're in. Since my husband Roy passed away it's just me and Audrey – who worked here as a Land Girl during the war – and my son Joe running the farm. And please call me Mary."

Audrey scratched at a sore patch of skin on her neck, her eyes a little hazy as she listened to the conversation. "I'll put a pot of tea on," she said, giving her head a little shake and snapping back to the present.

"Come round the back of the house to the scullery," said Mary, beginning to lead the way along a muddy path that hugged the side of the house. "Joe, can you fetch in Storm and put the cart of beets in the small barn?" she called, gesturing at the horse waiting patiently by the gate with the cart.

Ruth glanced back at Joe, who had ignored his mum's instruction and was standing stock still, watching them as he leaned on the pitchfork. He met Ruth's gaze. His eyes were like hot pokers, and to Ruth's surprise they seemed to be sending a clear message that said "leave and don't come back". Her stomach squirmed.

"Hurry up, Ruth," called her mum, who had picked up the suitcase and already set off after Mary.

Ruth half ran after her mum, feeling the heat of the boy's eyes stabbing into her back with every step.

Chapter 6

Not Welcome

In the tiled scullery, Ruth and her mum followed Mary's instructions to take off their wet shoes and drape their dripping coats over a wooden rack.

"Come through to the kitchen," Mary said, pulling off her peaked cap to reveal straw-coloured hair tied back into a rough plait. Her burnt-orange wool jumper was large, had several holes in and made her look smaller than she was.

The flagstones were cold under Ruth's damp socks, her feet leaving ghostly imprints as she followed Mary and her mum into the kitchen. A black range clicked gently on one wall, but the room still had a chill to it. Ruth heard the steady *drip-drip-drip* of the rain and looked to the window, then realized the sound was not coming from outside at all. It came from a tin pail positioned below the window to catch a leak from the sagging ceiling above. The wide fireplace was laid with small pieces of coal but unlit. Ruth's spirits dipped a little further. Coal was still rationed, and she supposed they must wait until the evening to light the fire, to avoid being wasteful. A line of washing pegged above the range filled the room with a mildly unpleasant aroma of wet wool. Below the washing, Dash lay on an old tartan rug. He bared his teeth and growled, but his tail thumped rhythmically on the floor. Ruth hoped that meant he wasn't about to bite her.

Audrey had pushed her thick jumper sleeves up to her elbows and was lighting two paraffin lamps. A silver charm bracelet she wore on her right wrist chimed like miniature church bells as she worked. "Sorry it's so dark in here. Same as everywhere else, we must try not to use electricity until later in the day. Even then it's hardly worth it, as we often get cuts in supply living out here," she said.

Ruth grimaced in sympathy. She found the electricity

shortages tiresome, especially in winter when the sun rose late and set early. Due to growing demand, the present advice meant the use of power should be avoided during the peak hours of the morning and afternoon. It meant that the electric fire in the living room wasn't switched on until almost teatime. Her mum had told her that, at the museum, people sometimes even resorted to working by candlelight.

"Please, sit yourselves down," wheezed Mary, gesturing at the large wooden table which was loaded with crates of what looked like bags of seeds. She picked up a box of matches and lit two thick waxy candles that were balanced on saucers in the centre of the table. Their flames wavered and jumped, as if dancing to a secretive breeze, and the gloom began to recede.

Ruth and her mum sat at the table and waited, watching Mary carry the crates through to the scullery. Mary winced as she lifted a particularly heavy crate and a volley of coughs burst from her mouth.

Ruth's mum sprang to her feet. "Here, let me help," she said, reaching over.

Mary shook her head firmly. "I'm all right. I can manage," she spluttered, placing a hand on her side.

The sound of the coughing made Ruth's stomach contract and her mum pressed her lips together in concern and sat down again.

Audrey ignored Mary's objections and lifted the remaining seed crates to the floor, then quickly wiped the dust from the table with a ragged cloth. Ruth's eyes were once again drawn to her charm bracelet. Her late grandmother had owned one quite similar and it was kept in her mum's jewellery box at home. Ruth coveted it and would often offer to polish it, her fingers gently roaming the bumps and curves of the artist's pallet, the trumpet and the impossibly tiny piano.

"You live in London then?" said Audrey, catching Ruth's eye as she folded the cloth.

Ruth nodded shyly.

"It must have been frightening being there during the war," said Audrey, her fingers absent-mindedly worrying at a tiny silver dancing shoe on her bracelet.

"It was," admitted Ruth.

"We survived, though. Luckily our home and the museum are still standing," said Ruth's mum.

"Did you live at Rook Farm all through the war?" asked Ruth, remembering that Mary had said Audrey worked as a Land Girl.

"Only towards the end of it. I worked on farms with the Women's Land Army, pulling potatoes and the like. That's how I met the Sterne family. Mary offered me work and a room here."

"You must have joined the Land Army when you were very young," said Ruth's mum.

"I'm twenty-four now. I came down from Norwich when I was sixteen, so I was younger than I should have been. But I certainly wasn't the only one to lie about my age in the war," said Audrey with a grimace.

"It must have been hard being away from your family," said Ruth, thinking about her friend Betty, who had not seen her family for four whole years during the war while she was evacuated. When she finally returned home, she'd regularly told Ruth that as soon as she was able, she intended to go back and live with her evacuee family in Devon, as they felt more like her family than her own. This idea still shocked Ruth each time she thought about it.

"I see my family once a month," replied Audrey. "Our terraced house in the city is still standing." Her face suddenly closed, as if a veil had been dropped over it.

The scullery door slammed shut, and Ruth heard low voices.

"I thought no one was coming from the museum. That's what you said," she heard a boy say. It had to be Joe.

"I didn't think anyone was coming, but I'm pleased I was mistaken," said Mary. "Have you settled Storm in the stable already?"

"Yes, I have." There was a short pause. "You need to tell those museum people to go, Mum," continued Joe in an urgent hiss.

"Shush, Joe, they'll hear you," replied Mary.

Audrey threw an anxious glance in the direction of the voices. "I'll make the tea," she said, heading for the pantry door.

Ruth and her mum shared an uncertain look. Why was Joe so unhappy at their arrival?

There was a crash and a yelp from the pantry.

"Oh dear," said Ruth's mum.

"I'll see if I can do anything to help," Ruth said, pushing back her chair. She found Audrey looking with dismay at a small broken jug on the floor, a river of milk pooling around it. "Silly me. I get clumsy when I'm tired," she said with a worn-out sigh.

"Can I do something?" asked Ruth.

"That's kind. You could fetch the cloth," said Audrey,

bending to pick up the broken china.

Joe and his mum were still whispering in the scullery. After fetching the cloth, Ruth paused outside. If she lingered for a second or two, maybe she would learn why Joe was being so unfriendly. But when he next spoke, Joe said something so unexpected Ruth smothered a gasp of pure indignation, her shoulders stiffening in shock.

CHAPTER 7

Whispers

Ruth hovered by the entrance to the scullery as Joe's words echoed in her ears. *"You shouldn't have invited those people here. They could be thieves, looking to make some money from what you've found. That young girl keeps giving me funny looks too. We don't need odd city folk like her and her mum snooping round our farm."*

Ruth's skin bristled and she glanced at her mum to see if she had heard, but she was busy rooting around in her rucksack. *Thieves?* How outrageous of him to suggest such a thing. And surely Joe was the one giving *her* funny looks – she couldn't be that much younger than he was. Ruth pushed her shoulders back and stood a little taller. She and her mum weren't any of the things Joe had said. They had come to help.

While Audrey mopped up the milk, Ruth offered to prepare the tea tray. Following Audrey's instructions on where to find everything, her mouth watered as she placed thick wedges of cherry cake on a plate. Carrying the tray to the table, Ruth could hear Joe in the scullery taking off his outdoor clothes and washing his hands as he whispered to his mum. Were they still talking about her?

"What a splendid cake. You must have all the fresh eggs and meat you need living here," Ruth's mum said, as Audrey set out the mugs and teaspoons.

"We do. We're lucky in that way. The cherries were tinned though, a present from my fiancé Terry. He likes bringing me little gifts," said Audrey, picking up the teapot. "We're getting married this summer."

"How nice," said Ruth's mum with a warm smile.

"What will you wear?" asked Ruth shyly, thinking of her friend Betty's older sister, who had made her own wedding dress out of parachute silk.

Audrey poured the tea. "I'll wear my mum's wedding dress. She'll like that. We don't have much money and

Terry can't afford to buy me an engagement ring, but I really don't mind."

Ruth looked up as Joe trailed behind his mum into the kitchen. Dash stood and stretched slowly. He padded over to Joe and looked up at him adoringly. But Joe ignored the dog and looked directly at Ruth, his gaze fierce and appraising, just as it had been outside. Shadows danced across his thick eyebrows and damp hair in the candlelight. He looked a little like a lion staking claim on his kingdom.

Ruth settled into her seat and took a sip of tea. He certainly wouldn't be getting any more "funny looks" from her because she would keep her face as blank as a sheet of paper from now on.

"I'm so grateful you've come to Rook Farm. I've been worried about what to do about my discovery," said Mary, taking a seat at the table and glancing at both Joe and Audrey. "I wish my Roy was here to advise me."

"My dad was interested in the old things he'd find in the fields," Joe explained, giving his mum a look that melted his hard face into something much softer and more pleasant. He nodded to the wooden dresser on the far wall of the kitchen. Ruth glanced at the shelves, surprised.

"You can look at them if you like," said Mary with a smile.

Curiosity caused Ruth to push back her chair and approach the dresser. Instead of china plates and mugs, she saw two small creamy-white animal skulls, a jumble of old penny coins, an arrowhead, and a fat lump of odd-shaped stone.

"These objects aren't valuable. They're things my Roy had a particular fondness for. Others he stored in our barn loft – I suppose it was his hobby of sorts. But he never found anything like what I found in the field two weeks ago," said Mary.

Ruth picked up the lump of stone and turned it over in her hand. It was gnarly, grey and fitted neatly in her palm.

"That's a coprolite," said Joe. "They used to be mined to make fertilizer around here. It's fossilized animal dung."

"Joe," exclaimed Audrey in disgust. Mary gave him a stern look and Joe looked a little sheepish.

Ruth ignored Joe, placed the dung down and wiped her hands on her trousers, the warmth in her cheeks betraying her intention to keep her face expressionless. "What did you find two weeks ago?" Ruth asked Mary, itching to know the reason for their visit.

"Yes, can we talk about your discovery, Mary? The done thing is to contact a local museum or the Ministry of Works within two weeks if you think you've made an important find," said Ruth's mum.

Mary coughed and rubbed at her chest. Her nails were short, stubby and encrusted with dirt. They made Ruth's mum's own short nails seem positively glamorous in comparison. "I heard Mr Knight interviewed on the wireless about the treasure found near here a few years back at Mildenhall. He was so knowledgeable that his name stuck with me. It seemed right to contact him when I found what I did," she said, pulling a handkerchief from her pocket and blowing her nose. "I'm sorry if I didn't do things the right way."

Ruth returned to the table and stood behind her mum. "The Mildenhall treasure is Roman and on display in the British Museum – I've seen it. There's a silver platter that's as wide as a door," she said flinging out her arms to emphasize just how big it was. She glanced at Joe and was pleased to see he looked a little impressed by this fact.

Ruth's mum leaned forward. "Those Roman finds from Mildenhall are one of the most substantial treasure troves ever to be uncovered in this country."

"What's a treasure trove?" asked Joe, his nose wrinkling.

"It's coins, gold or silver, buried in the ground," said Ruth's mum. "If someone has buried a treasure trove and hasn't returned for it then it can be claimed by the landowner, and whoever finds it, as long as they have permission to be on the land."

"Oh," said Joe, chewing on his bottom lip.

"Have you…found something like that?" asked Ruth a little hesitantly. The damp air in the kitchen suddenly felt thicker than ever and she held her breath. The Mildenhall treasure had been the talk of London, photographs of it filling the pages of every national newspaper and magazine that her mum had pored over obsessively. Over thirty pieces of Roman tableware – silver platters and dishes and spoons – had been discovered by a farmer in Suffolk during the war and put on display in the British Museum just the previous year. The largest silver platter was engraved with scenes from the ocean – dolphins, seahorses, and scallop shells. It drew big crowds at the museum. The thought of Mary finding something like that in her fields made the hairs on Ruth's arms stand on end.

"I'll tell you from the beginning. I was ploughing

Rook Field when I found it," began Mary.

"Rook Field?" interrupted Ruth's mum, who was busy recording the conversation in her notebook.

"All the fields on our farm have names. Rook Field, Marsh Field, House Field, Magpie, Gull and Eel and so on. Anyhow, I was ploughing deeper than usual, preparing the soil for spring planting. I was looking behind at the furrows and saw something lying on a clod of soil." Mary nodded at the dresser. "Fetch it, will you, Joe?"

Joe's eyes narrowed and for a moment Ruth thought he was going to refuse. He roughly pushed back his tawny hair and strode to the dresser. Pulling open one of the cupboard doors, he took out a small object wrapped in hessian sacking. He cradled it in his palms, as if he was holding something very precious that he coveted all for himself.

Ruth drew in a breath, her fingers tingling in anticipation of what they were about to see.

"Joe?" said Mary.

Joe looked up. "Mum...I don't..."

"Just bring it here and show it to Harriett and Ruth," Mary said, her voice soft yet exasperated.

Joe did as his mum asked and stood watching as

Ruth's mum carefully peeled back the layers of sacking and drew in a sharp breath.

Ruth leaned over her mum's shoulder to better see the treasure that had led them all the way from London to the Fens. She swallowed a gasp of surprise as she realized this was not what she had been expecting to see at all.

CHAPTER 8

Piperatorium

"What is it?" asked Ruth, looking at the silver gilt object sitting on the table in front of them.

"It's extraordinary, that's what it is," breathed Ruth's mum.

"Is it?" asked Mary, her voice high with hope.

The small silver statue was about the length of an outstretched hand. It had been fashioned in the form of a woman's head and upper torso. Her hair was parted in the middle, and she wore a bead necklace and wide-sleeved tunic with engraved decorations on the shoulders. Ruth saw she was holding something in her left hand, perhaps a scroll which she was gesturing towards with two pointed fingers. She was tinged with green and bore traces of dark soil in her folds and crevices, but despite this, the engraving was so intricate that Ruth thought the object looked recently made, rather than from centuries ago.

Ruth glanced at Joe and saw his cheeks were quite pale as he stared at the statue. Was he worrying that her mum was going to swipe it from the table and run off with it? She frowned.

Audrey stood watching quietly, her back to the range. She sipped her tea, her eyes fixed on Ruth's mum.

"You think this is important…that it could be worth something?" asked Mary haltingly, smothering a cough.

"This is a silver *piperatorium*, a roman pepper pot," said Ruth's mum, high spots of colour flaming her cheeks. "Roman tableware is very rare, not often found in this country, or anywhere for that matter."

"A pepper pot. But I can't see any holes for the pepper to come out?" said Ruth.

Joe nibbled on a thumbnail and leaned over to look too.

Ruth watched as her mum carefully turned the statue upside down. "You see this circular disc on the base?

This would turn to allow the pepper to be shaken out, or for the pot to be refilled. This object is made of silver because it holds something rather valuable – the Romans considered pepper an exotic spice. It really is quite astonishing and of great historical value."

"But is the pot valuable?" asked Mary insistently, placing her hands flat on the table.

Ruth's mum looked up. "Yes, I think it is. But there would be many steps to go through before you saw any money from its sale. Treasure is usually presented to a valuation committee and only then can a museum offer to buy it. The process can take many months."

"Months?" said Audrey, her forehead crinkling. She glanced at Mary, who looked crestfallen.

"There's no way to hurry up the process?" asked Mary hopefully.

Ruth's mum looked apologetic. "Things need to be done the proper way I'm afraid."

Audrey and Mary exchanged a disappointed look.

Ruth remembered what Mary had said on the telephone about the treasure perhaps saving her farm from ruin. It did seem to be in a tumbledown state outside and in, and she could see they needed money for repairs. "You're sure it's Roman?" she asked, focusing again on the pepper pot. Aside from the greenish hue, she was unable to shake from her head the newness of the object. How was it possible for something to look so good after centuries of being buried in a field?

"Yes, I'm certain. I have seen an item like this before at the museum. Did you clean it yourself, Mary?" asked her mum. Ruth saw a lightning-quick shadow flicker across her mum's face.

"A little, just to get the worst of the peat off. I was careful," Mary said, smothering a cough.

"I'm sure you were," said Ruth's mum, who still seemed a little puzzled by something.

"How old is it?" asked Mary curiously.

"I couldn't be sure exactly. A find can be difficult to date unless coins are found alongside it, which bear a date and the name of the emperor of the time," said Ruth's mum, carefully placing the pepper pot on the hessian. "But I'd say it's likely to be from the fourth century, which makes it over one thousand years old."

"Goodness," said Ruth. "I think the woman's clothes and necklace are very grand. They make her look a little like an empress or a queen."

"Yes, she does have an imperious look about her,"

said Ruth's mum with a smile. "Objects like this are often part of a larger set of tableware." She looked up at Mary, her eyes gleaming. "What else did you find in the field?"

"Mum," said Joe in a low voice which sounded a little like a warning.

Mary ignored Joe and nodded. "I think there were other items buried, but I was scared to dig around in case I damaged them. I decided the best thing was to leave the area undisturbed and unmarked, to protect the things. I hope I did the right thing?"

"But you do recall the exact spot where you discovered the pepper pot?" asked Ruth's mum, her face expectant. Her fingers twitched at her sides as if already anticipating the feel of the handle of her trowel scraping across the soil and searching objects out. Ruth felt a strong desire to get outside and start digging too.

"I memorized the number of paces to the spot... didn't tell a soul, not even Joe," said Mary.

Ruth noticed a slow flush creeping up Joe's neck. He pulled at the collar of his thick jumper. Any mention of the treasure made him strangely uncomfortable.

"I must go out to the field at once, if I may? I brought my tools, but it would be useful to borrow a bucket, some shovels and planks of wood, if you have any to hand?" said Ruth's mum eagerly. "We'll also need a small crate to bring back anything we find."

Ruth saw Joe glance doubtfully at the raindrops tracking down the window. "You want to go out in this weather?" he said.

"I imagine you and your mum work in all weathers too? A little rain will never deter an archaeologist," said Ruth's mum with a wry smile.

Joe nodded but didn't return her smile.

"Joe, you go and find Harriett whatever she needs. Audrey, can you put some extra dumplings in the stew? Harriett and Ruth must stay for tea this evening," said Mary.

"Oh no, really, we don't want to intrude," said Ruth's mum. "We'll return to Ely to find a bed and breakfast. There was one by the station that had vacancies. We just need to know the time of the last bus that passes the end of the farm track."

"I shan't hear of it," said Mary, shaking her head firmly. "In fact, Audrey, please make up the spare room for our guests. The two of you will have to share a bed, mind, but it's the least I can do to repay you for coming all this way."

Ruth tried her best to hide her dismay. An overnight stay in this cold and isolated farmhouse would save money, but it would not be as pleasant as a cosy bed and breakfast. And as Joe's eyebrows arched with displeasure she thought he wasn't too impressed at having them as house guests either.

In the excitement of their unexpected trip to Rook Farm, Ruth and her mum had forgotten to bring their rubber boots. Fortunately, Mary had an impressive assortment in the scullery and told them to help themselves. All the boots Ruth tried on were slightly too big and her still-damp socks slopped around in them uncomfortably, but this did nothing to quell her excitement at finally being outside and on the way to see what else Mary had discovered.

As they set off across the ploughed field behind the house, Ruth wiped the drizzle from her eyes and tightened her grip on the bucket she was carrying. Her mum and Mary stalked ahead across the rutted soil with the rucksack of tools, shovels and the small wooden crate for bringing any finds back to the house.

The land was so flat and the clouds so grey, that the

field and sky seemed to merge into one. Aside from the farm, there wasn't a single other building in sight and the only sounds were the hum of the wind, the splatter of rain on the mud and their feet stomping on the ground. The contrast with the busyness of London and its constant streams of people and noise was startling. Ruth wondered what her friend Betty was doing in London right now. Perhaps reading her fortnightly copy of *The Dandy Comic*, which they would often giggle over in the school playground. She couldn't wait to tell Betty about her visit to the farm – a treasure hunt no less!

Joe walked a few paces to Ruth's left, two short wooden planks wedged under one arm. His dog trotted slowly beside him. Dash whimpered and came to a halt and Joe bent to stroke his head and fondle his ears. "Come on, old boy. It's cold, but a bit of fresh air will do you good." Joe's voice was full of warmth and affection, quite different from the way he had spoken back at the house.

"Why did you call him Dash?" Ruth asked, thinking that if she was friendlier to Joe he might be friendlier in return.

Joe looked up. "He has this white line of fur between his eyes. Dad said it looked like a dash. Mum said one of Queen Victoria's favourite dogs went by that name and that decided it."

"The name suits him," said Ruth with a smile.

Joe gave her a curt nod and walked on.

Ruth took a deep breath as they approached a small wooden bridge crossing a water-filled ditch. Perhaps if she chatted to Joe a little about her life it would prove he had no need to be suspicious of her or her mum. "I suppose you're on school holidays this week like me?" she asked.

Joe nodded, his boots thumping over the soil.

"What do you usually do in the holidays? Sometimes my friend Betty and I go to the pictures," said Ruth. "*The Wizard of Oz* is our favourite; we've seen it at least five times."

Joe gave her a sidelong glance. "I do the same thing I always do in the holidays. Work on the farm and help Mum."

Ruth frowned. "But you can't work all the time."

Joe laughed. It was a sour and unhappy sound. "Mum and the farm need me, and I haven't time for anything else because of…" His voice trailed off and he looked shifty, as if he had been about to say something he might later regret.

"Because of what?" asked Ruth curiously.

"Nothing," said Joe sullenly. "How long will you be here?" His sudden question was direct and loaded with confrontation. Ruth suddenly felt bowed with weariness from their journey, the rain, the biting wind and this odd boy.

"When is your dad expecting you home?" Joe asked, his breath pluming into the air.

Ruth lowered her head and stamped on a particularly large clod of earth. "He's not," she said quickly, wishing to draw the conversation to a close. She yanked her knitted hat over her ears, which smarted with cold, and wiped the rain from her face.

"Oh. He's passed on too?" said Joe, his voice suddenly looser and softer than before. "I'm…sorry about that."

Ruth's cheeks felt tight and waxy. She did not have the energy to correct him or want to share her family's problems. "Mum, wait!" she called. Her boots slipped and slid in the furrows and the bucket swung in her hand as she ran across the bridge and after her mum, putting as much distance between herself and Joe as she could.

Chapter 9

Excavation

Ruth's gloves were itchy and damp and Joe's questions about her dad made her think of home. An unexpected rush of tears built behind her eyes, and she blinked them away. She thought of her dad sitting alone in London in his sparsely furnished flat. "I'll soon make it feel like home," he had said to Ruth brightly, after she had blurted out her dismay at how strange the flat was, while they'd been having tea and biscuits a week ago. It didn't feel like a home – not her home anyway – and she couldn't see how it ever would. Her parents' divorce had turned everything upside down and inside out and she sometimes had to stamp on any rising feelings of resentment.

"Everything all right?" her mum asked now, glancing at Ruth as she placed her rucksack on the damp, peaty soil. She opened the flap and pulled out the two cake-slice-shaped trowels, a length of twine and a handful of small wooden stakes.

"Everything's fine," said Ruth, pushing thoughts of her parents' divorce to one side and plonking the bucket down. She was intrigued to see what they might find and did not want to distract her mum from the task she had come here to do. They were going home tomorrow and she would never see Joe again, so she didn't need to be friends with him.

"Please place the planks next to my rucksack for now, Joe," said Ruth's mum, glancing at her watch. "It's just after three o'clock. It will be dark in a couple of hours – we need to get cracking."

Ruth busied herself by rooting around in the rucksack for her mum's battered field notebook and pencil. She felt Dash nudge her side and flinched. His dark eyes looked at her expectantly and his tail swished from side to side, raindrops clinging to it like tiny glass beads. Ruth moved away, still wary of the dog.

Ruth's mum took off her gloves and crouched to examine the sticky soil. She felt it between her fingers as if she was sifting flour to make a cake. "I've never worked with soil as dark and rich as this," she said, her voice clear and light.

"What happens now?" asked Mary. She was standing on the exact spot in Rook Field where she had found the pepper pot, marking it like a cross on a treasure map.

"Well, I'll use my compass to determine which way is north, then use the stakes and twine to mark out a box around the area where you are standing. This will be where we'll dig. If there are more things to be found, it is important the site is excavated properly, and the items recorded in my notebook," said Ruth's mum, assembling her tools in the way an accomplished cook brings together ingredients in the kitchen.

Ruth felt a swell of pride as her mum confidently pushed the small stakes into the soil at intervals to mark out the square. "What can I do?" she asked.

Ruth's mum looked up. "If you could twist the twine round the stakes and Joe could lay the planks, that would be a great help."

Joe gave a nod, but his lips were downturned.

Dash nuzzled his legs and whimpered again.

Ruth crouched and began the task of winding the twine around the short stakes as Mary retold the tale of how and where she had found the pepper pot. She stopped midway, consumed by a coughing fit, the sound echoing into the gloomy sky.

Ruth's nose dripped as she worked, and she paused to wipe it on the back of a glove.

A white handkerchief suddenly dropped in front of her eyes. She blinked and looked up.

"Take it," said Joe, shaking the handkerchief.

Ruth sat back on her heels and looked at it for a second or two. He waved it again. It was almost like a flag of truce. She stood up, took the handkerchief and blew her nose, then held it out to him.

His lips lifted into a sudden smile which lit up his face. "Best keep it until it's had a wash."

She felt a burn of embarrassment and stuffed it into her coat pocket. "Thank you."

"Dad didn't enlist during the war because farming was a reserved occupation. But he died anyway during last summer's harvest. Doctor said he had a bad heart." The words from Joe's lips were so quiet and unexpected Ruth wondered at first if she had imagined them.

The wind gusted and Joe shoved his hands into his coat pockets.

"You must miss him," said Ruth, glancing at Mary and her mum, who were still talking a short distance away.

Joe nodded. "There's not much time to think about it though, what with the farm to look after, and Mum." He paused. "I'm sorry if asking about your dad upset you."

Ruth looked above Joe's head as four geese flew in formation, honking loudly. "My dad just doesn't live with us any more. My parents are divorcing."

"Oh," said Joe, throwing her a sympathetic look.

Some of Ruth's friends' parents had also decided to separate having grown apart during the war; this knowledge had given Ruth a strange and unhappy relief that her family weren't the only ones going through changes. All the same it brought a sad twist to her stomach whenever she spoke about it. She took in again the vastness of the fields and the farmhouse, now small in the distance, and thought about what Joe had said about his own dad. "You and your mum don't manage *all* of this land alone, do you?"

Joe shrugged. "My older brother Billy left when the

war was over. People are leaving the land in droves to work in the towns and cities now. Billy works in a stable yard in Newmarket and has a steady girlfriend. He doesn't visit much."

"That must be hard on you and your mum," said Ruth, bending to wind the twine round the final stake.

Joe swiped the rain from his face. "Billy made his choice. Mum and Dad might not have liked it, but they accepted it. My choice is to be here with Mum and run the farm myself one day."

"Joe. Please can you do as Harriett asked and lay the planks?" called Mary.

Joe's shoulders tightened, as if unhappy about being pulled back into the present. "What are the planks for?" he asked.

"We can kneel on them to stop our knees getting soggy. If we have to dig deep we can also use them to prop up the sides of the trench and stop the soil collapsing," Ruth's mum replied.

"You won't have to dig deep," said Joe quickly, picking up a plank and following Harriett's directions for where to lay it.

Ruth frowned. "How do you know that?"

"I mean…Mum said the pepper pot was found near

the surface of the soil, didn't you, Mum?" said Joe, his cheeks mottled pink.

"It was," confirmed Mary.

"Well in that case I think we'll use the trowels to excavate, rather than dig with the shovels," said Ruth's mum.

With the planks in place, Ruth handed her mum the field notebook.

Her mum opened it to a new page and swiftly drew a series of lines and numbers.

"What are you doing?" asked Mary, walking over.

"Mum's making a map of the site," said Ruth.

Ruth's mum nodded. "This arrow I've drawn marks north, and the square below is the area we'll dig. I'll record here anything we find. See this line and number? The line is the field boundary, and the number means the paces walked."

"How clever," said Mary, peering at the book. She held her side as she leaned over and puffed out a small groan which turned into a coughing fit.

"Are you sure you shouldn't be inside?" said Ruth's mum, looking up.

Mary continued to cough but waved a hand dismissively.

Joe hovered at the edge of the marked-out area, his features strained as he watched his mum. Dash snuffled at the planks and sneezed.

Ruth's mum pushed the notebook into her pocket and picked up the trowel. She held the second one out to Joe with a smile. "You have a go at excavating alongside me. Start at this end of the square and use the long edge of the trowel to scrape a thin layer of earth towards you." She paused. "But please don't try and do this on your own without me being here, Joe. It could do more harm than good."

"Oh…no, I mustn't," said Joe. He was looking at the trowel as if it were a weapon, something to be feared.

"Go on," urged Ruth. "It's your land. Imagine how you'll feel if you find something important."

Joe shook his head again and bent to stroke Dash, who was quivering. "I'll take Dash back to the house. His bones ache if he's out in the wet for too long."

Ruth nodded. "Maybe you could come back afterwards?"

Joe gave her a non-committal shrug.

"Do you want a go at excavating, Ruth?" asked her mum, offering her the trowel instead.

Ruth grinned, feeling a surge of excitement. She kneeled on the plank, the cold and damp wood seeping through her trousers. Dipping her head, she used the trowel to scrape the soil towards her, just like her mum was doing. The earth was sticky and quickly stained her woollen gloves, but she was so absorbed in the task she didn't care one small bit.

Ruth sensed Joe still as a statue to her right, silently watching. Mary was quiet too. The only sounds were the spatter of the rain, the whoosh of the wind, Dash's occasional whine and the scrape of metal on dirt. After a while, Ruth looked up and straightened the crick in her neck. She saw Joe give his dog an absent-minded pat – he seemed to have forgotten all about taking Dash back to the house.

The small mound of excavated soil began to grow, and Ruth used a shovel to scoop it into a bucket. As she did, she heard the thin scrape of her mum's trowel striking something solid.

Ruth's mum sucked in a breath, leaned forward and continued to carefully clear the ploughed soil away from the thing she had found.

Ruth, Joe and Mary gathered round her in a tight huddle.

"Look," said Ruth, pointing to something long and thin emerging from the peat.

Joe quickly dropped to his knees. He reached for the object and wiped away some of the cloying mud. It looked like a long, slim-handled cooking spoon.

"Careful, Joe," exclaimed Mary.

"This is…quite unbelievable," Ruth's mum said, reaching for a second and then a third similar-shaped object. "I think they are silver cooking ladles." She used a finger to scoop earth from one of the ladle's bowls, then her handkerchief to polish them a little. She squinted. "There's an engraved inscription. It says… Octavius."

Ruth felt a flare of recognition. "Isn't that a Roman name?"

"Yes. These objects are Roman. I am sure of it." Ruth's mum turned to Mary, her eyes glimmering. "I think you've unearthed a treasure trove on your land."

"Treasure!" exclaimed Ruth with a grin.

Mary's smile stretched from ear to ear. "Well I never," she wheezed. "These things are likely to be valuable then?"

Ruth's mum grinned and nodded. "The British Museum will certainly be very interested."

Ruth glanced at Joe, expecting to see a similar look of glee. But instead his lips were drawn into a hard line and his eyes seemed to be swimming with alarm as he stared at the ladle in his hand.

Chapter 10

Secret

As Ruth's mum used a tape measure to help record the position of the three ladles on the plan she had drawn in her notebook, Ruth continued to excavate the site, all the while puzzling over why Joe had looked at the treasure with such alarm. It made little sense, for surely he should be pleased this treasure had been found on their land, when its sale could help support the farm.

Joe passed the ladle he had been holding to Ruth's mum without saying a word and started for the house with Dash, his face tight and unreadable, his pace quickening with every step.

Mary left soon after, her cheeks pallid as the drizzle misted the landscape to a grey blur. "Well, this is exciting. I'd like to stay, but I mustn't get behind with pulling up the beets ready for taking to the sugar factory. The weather's supposed to worsen, perhaps snow in the next few days, which will mean work will have to stop."

Ruth looked up at Mary in surprise. "Sugar factory?"

Mary smiled and pointed over Ruth's shoulder. "Half this country's sugar comes from beet growing on farms like ours. It's what kept us going in the war." Her eyes darkened and she shook her head. "Only problem is I can't afford to pay workers to come and pull it from the ground any more. Maybe this treasure find will help with that, though it seems it might be a while before we get any money for it."

Ruth turned, looking in the direction Mary had pointed. Beyond another ditch, leafy green plant fronds grew in uniform lines in the neighbouring field. There had to be hundreds, if not thousands of them. How could Mary, Joe and Audrey tend to all these plants without workers to help them?

"I'll see you back at the house. Audrey will have tea on the table at five o'clock," Mary said, striding off, her hacking coughs echoing behind her.

Ruth glanced at her watch. Tea was in one hour and after that it would be dark. They didn't have much time to finish the excavation. She pushed all her energy into her trowel, hoping against hope to uncover something else important.

As the dull afternoon faded to dusk, Ruth's mum eventually stood up, gazed at the growing mound of excavated soil and said it was time to call it a day.

Gingerly picking up the silver ladles from the crate, Ruth examined each in turn as her mum packed up her tools. Octavius's name was engraved onto each small ladle bowl. Two dolphins sat either side of the ladles' handles, their heads curving outwards. To think these were from Roman times! Who was Octavius? Had he eaten or prepared food with these ladles? It gave her a peculiar thrill to think she was one of the first people to have held these objects in over one thousand years. Her only slight regret was that she hadn't found anything herself.

As they prepared to walk back across the field, Ruth's mum turned and looked at the site, deep in thought.

"What's wrong?" asked Ruth, holding the crate of ladles close to her body.

"Nothing," her mum said, but she sounded uncertain.

"Why would these things have been buried here, Mum?" asked Ruth, thinking that choosing this large, flat field to bury such precious items seemed a bit peculiar.

"Times were turbulent in fourth-century Italy, and the Romans living in Britain returned home to help defend their empire. They buried their tableware and coins, probably to keep them safe until they could come back," said her mum, pulling her torch from her rucksack. She stood and directed the beam of light at the darkening trenches they had dug, a puzzled expression still clouding her face.

"So you think that's why the pepper pot and ladles were buried here?" asked Ruth, picturing a man in a Roman tunic burying the items in the dead of night. The past was pulling vividly into the present and it made her shiver.

"Perhaps," said her mum, still looking thoughtful.

"Come on, Mum. We don't want to be late for tea," said Ruth, stamping her feet against the chill.

"Um. I think I might stay out here a little longer," her mum replied slowly.

"But it's getting dark," said Ruth in surprise. "Audrey will have tea ready."

"I know. I just want to check a few things. I'll come back to the house with you and ask Audrey to keep my tea warm in the range. I'll also see if there is a bigger torch I can borrow," her mum replied.

Ruth's mum set off for the house, her feet sure and steady across the ruts and dips of the field as she led the way.

Ruth hurried to keep up, her boots sliding in the thick mud. Her mum was behaving a bit strangely, as if she had a problem she didn't know the answer to. "What's bothering you? Is it something about the ladles?" asked Ruth, thinking again of Joe's alarm at their discovery.

Her mum was quiet for a long moment. "I just want to be thorough. Mr Knight and the museum would expect that of me, especially if I am to get a job there," she said eventually, her torch beam flaring in the mist like a comet's tail.

Her mum mentioning Mr Knight and the job made Ruth's mind turn, unbidden, to London and home again. It was the house where she had fallen and cut her chin on a table and her dad had sung silly songs to distract her. It was the house her dad and mum had been happy in once, their laughter like a warm blanket as Ruth drifted off to sleep in her bedroom. As she strode beside her mum across the field, her jaw clenched at the thought of moving somewhere new and leaving these memories behind. She sucked in a deep breath, the air so bitter it burned the inside of her nose and brought tears to her eyes.

Ruth stood at the scullery window and watched her mum stride back across the fields to the excavation site with the larger torch she had found in the scullery. Why was she so insistent on working in the dark? It felt to Ruth as if she was being secretive.

Leaving the crate of ladles on the draining board, Ruth pulled off her muddy boots, sodden coat and gloves and peeped into the kitchen. There had been no one in when they'd returned from the field, the house dark and still. But the air was heavy with the smell of over-cooked meat, as if something was on the brink of burning.

Dash lay on his blanket and gave a low growl in Ruth's direction. He had barked aggressively when she and her mum had approached the house, the sound making Ruth's stomach tighten. Where was everyone? She walked briskly through the kitchen to the hallway, giving Dash an extra wide berth. He snarled again, but she also heard his tail thump on the floor.

In the hallway she peered up the stairs into the gloom. "Hello," she called tentatively. There was no reply. The front door bumped, and she whirled round. The wind wailed and hummed. Another swirling gust caused the door to shudder. The gathering darkness was suddenly oppressive, leaching inside through the cracks and crevices. Ruth thought of the long track leading to the road. This kind of isolation was new and unnerving.

Quickly retracing her steps into the kitchen, Ruth glanced to the window overlooking the yard. The door to the biggest of the barns was open, a faint light spilling onto the wet concrete. The burning smell from the range was becoming pungent. She needed to tell someone.

Swiftly pulling on her boots again, Ruth ran round the side of the house and across the yard. Ducking into the barn she blinked as her eyes adjusted to the low light. She saw the dim outline of tools hanging on the walls, spades and forks and strange implements she didn't know the names of. Towards the back of the barn sat a small tractor. The place smelled damp, of muck and hay.

A thud above her head made her look up. The light she had seen from the kitchen window bled through gaps in the rafters.

"Why did this happen? It's such a muddle," a voice muttered.

It was Joe. She should alert him to the fact she was lurking down there, and about the burning food, but something made her pause. A rustling noise came from above and she wondered what he was doing and who he was talking to. Curiosity drew her slowly towards a ladder leading to the loft.

"This secret…it's too big. I wish you were here, Dad. You'd know how to make things right," Joe said in a low voice.

Joe was having an imaginary conversation with his dad. *What was his secret?* Ruth bit hard on her lower lip. She placed one foot on the bottom rung of the ladder, hoping to hear more. Climbing stealthily upwards, she heard a sudden whump. It sounded very much like a metal lid being slammed shut. Then the quick thud of feet on wood.

Torchlight dazzled Ruth's eyes. She blinked, her feet wobbling.

Joe swung the torch away from her face as he peered down, his eyes wide in shock. "What are you doing up here?"

Ruth curled her fingers round the edges of the ladder. "Um…something is burning in the range. Everyone was out. Didn't you hear me call?" She swallowed back an arrow of guilt at the lie.

The shock on Joe's face smoothed away. "Tell Audrey. She gets forgetful when there's a lot to do. She's feeding the cows in the shed behind the stables."

Ruth edged back down the ladder, her brain buzzing like flies trapped in a jar as she wondered what secret Joe was keeping. It sounded like he had been looking at something in the hayloft, something he didn't want anyone else to know about.

CHAPTER 11

Knock at the Door

Joe was quiet and subdued during tea and Ruth watched him carefully, thinking about the secret she had heard him mention in the barn loft and wondering what it could be. She felt shy sitting at a table with this unfamiliar family, though Mary and Audrey did their utmost to make her feel welcome, including her in conversations and asking about their lives in London during the war.

Ruth tightened her grip on her knife and fork as she spoke of her mum's work as a dispatch rider, ferrying important, and sometimes top secret, documents across London on her bicycle to help the war effort. This had become increasingly difficult during the Blitz when whole streets were devastated by fallen bombs and everyone was on high alert for air raids. Sometimes her mum had worked at night and Ruth remembered being taken by their neighbour Mrs Drake into the Underground station to shelter when the sirens blared. She recalled absorbing the thud of the bombs into her bones, as she lay on the narrow metal bunk, breathing in smells of sweat and urine, listening to a man cheerfully playing the accordion as a distraction for the hundreds of people cowering below ground while the ceiling shuddered and dust fell like rain. She would curl on her side and wonder if her mum was safe cycling the streets and if her dad was in danger on his ship. Ruth remembered one occasion when her mum had been cycling across Bloomsbury after a particularly bad bombing raid and seen that the British Museum, where she had just started work as a volunteer, was on fire. She had stood and watched helplessly as the fire wardens used golf clubs to clear the incendiary bombs falling onto the roof of the museum before they caught light and engulfed it in flames. Ruth had been eager for details but also fearful for her mum's safety and the loss of buildings and streets in the London she knew and loved.

Mary listened open-mouthed as Ruth recounted these stories and Audrey sat back in her seat listening avidly.

"You all go up to bed," Audrey said as soon as they had all scraped the last of the slightly blackened, but satisfying, stew from their plates.

"I'll help clear up first," said Ruth, glancing at her watch. It was just after six thirty, which she felt was very early to be going to bed, especially in the school holidays.

Mary took another sip of water to help suppress a coughing fit. Ruth saw Audrey and Joe exchange an anxious look. It had to be hard being ill when there was such physical and demanding work to do. Ruth supposed you couldn't take a day off and, in order to get better, lie in bed with a warm lemon-and-honey drink. She noticed that Mary didn't protest at turning in so early. She just said a quick goodnight and headed for the stairs.

As Ruth stacked plates and carried them to the scullery sink, she wondered again how long her mum would be outside. She didn't want to go up to bed alone. She realized how odd it must have been for her evacuated friends, being flung together with a new family with the expectation they would just make the best of things. She glanced out of the scullery window and saw the flicker of her mum's torch in the dark. She must be hungry, but something was keeping her out there.

"Why hasn't your mum come in yet?" Joe's words echoed Ruth's thoughts, but they were as prickly as porcupine spines as he peered out into the dark too.

"I...don't know," admitted Ruth, drying a plate and placing it on the draining board next to the crate of silver ladles.

"Does she always work at night?" persisted Joe, folding his arms. The lights in the scullery flickered. The wind shuddered the glass panes, as if someone was outside rattling them.

Audrey picked up the stack of dried plates and Ruth saw her eyes skim across the ladles. They glinted as the electric light above brightened and dimmed. The house lights pulsed once more, then extinguished without warning.

The shock of being plunged into darkness made the cutlery Ruth was now drying slip from her fingers and clatter to the tiled floor. Dash growled and fussed around her legs. Ruth stood as still as a statue, raising her hands in case the dog nibbled her fingers. She blinked again and again as she listened to Audrey settling Dash and searching for matches.

Then came the welcome sound of a match striking, and the flicker of light. Ruth blinked once more as her eyes adjusted to the ghostly glow from a molten candle on the scullery windowsill. She looked around. Joe had disappeared. How had he managed to do that so silently and in the dark? Ruth shivered, trying to feel brave about spending a night in this cold and isolated house.

They had finished clearing up and, with no sign of her mum coming inside and Audrey off to bed, Ruth accepted she would have to turn in for the night too.

"These cuts in electricity remind me of the war and the blackouts," Audrey said, passing Ruth a hot-water bottle, then picking up a paraffin lamp and gesturing for Ruth to follow.

Ruth glanced at the note Audrey had left for her mum on the kitchen table, telling her where to find her plate of stew and the room they would be sleeping in.

She swallowed a quell of annoyance at being left alone all evening and followed Audrey up the stairs, along the landing and into a room at the far end.

The room was sparsely decorated, a table to the right of the bed, and a chest of drawers to the left. The curtains at the window were lined with heavy blackout material. The air was damp and cold and Ruth felt the room hadn't seen visitors for a very long time.

Audrey placed the lamp on a bedside table while Ruth slipped the rubber hot-water bottle under the sheets. It seemed Audrey had already brought up their small suitcase, which stood at the foot of the bed.

"It must have been horrid living in London during the Blitz," Audrey said. As she looked at Ruth, her fingers worried at the charms on her bracelet.

A sudden memory of whistling bombs and bright flashes of light flew into Ruth's head. The war might have finished two and a half years ago, but talking about it over tea had made her realize she could not remember a time before it. Normal life was queuing at the corner shop for rations of undersized eggs and a pint of milk that was supposed to last a full week. Normal life was often dining on mutton and mash in large dining halls because it was cheaper than cobbling together a meal with the provisions they had at home. Normal life was brown sticky tape across the windows in case a bomb blew them in, or queuing early for a place to sleep in the safety of the underground station. But through all the worries and hardships, Ruth's mum had remained positive and determined. She'd ensured that Ruth attended school every day, even after the school suffered bomb damage and lessons had to be relocated to a nearby church.

"We got through the war like everyone did, I suppose, but it's over now," said Ruth.

"I'm glad it's over," said Audrey. "But if the war hadn't happened, I would never have come here and met my fiancé Terry. Don't you think life is funny like that? A turn of a coin and your life changes for ever? It's important to try and be optimistic."

"It is," agreed Ruth.

"I have to keep positive for Terry. He hires young people to work on the farms around here. During the war he had over a hundred men and girls working for him. He has less than a quarter of that number now," continued Audrey.

"Is that because people are moving to the towns and cities?" asked Ruth, remembering what Joe had said about his brother Billy leaving the farm.

"That's right. Terry lives with his mum in the next village along. He comes here to help out when he can. After we're married in the summer we'll most likely live with his mum."

"Your family must be excited about the wedding," said Ruth.

Audrey scratched at her neck. "It will be a small do. I'm not sure they'll be able to come. Mum and Dad are working all hours at the shoe factory and my sister Emma is preparing to get married too. Her fiancé's a lovely chap. They've no money, but they're...so very happy." Her final words came out in a long slow breath. Audrey rubbed her neck again, as if she had an itch she could not satisfy. "What do you think your mum will do next? With the treasure I mean. Will she take it back to London?"

Ruth shook her head, thinking that Audrey looked a little anxious. "I don't know. You'd have to ask her." She glanced towards the window, and the light that still bobbed out in the field.

The sound of Dash's barks echoed up the stairs, cutting through their conversation. Someone was knocking at the front door. Audrey glanced at her wristwatch. "It's late for visitors." Picking up the torch she had brought with her, she turned and hurried down the landing. Ruth heard Mary come from her room and exchange a few words with Audrey, before going downstairs.

Then, the sound of raised voices and another volley of rapid barks from Dash.

Ruth crept along the gloomy landing, curious to see what the commotion was. She paused at the top of the stairs and leaned over the banister. Joe was standing in red plaid pyjamas on a step halfway down nibbling on a thumbnail.

"You're not welcome here," Ruth heard Mary say, her voice high with agitation.

Ruth winced at the rattle coming from her throat.

"You're a stubborn fool, Mary Sterne," said a man. His voice was thin and it sent a shiver down Ruth's back.

"Just leave. I won't have you filling Joe's head with talk of tractors and machinery. You've no right coming here and interfering with our business," said Mary. "Keep off my land from now on."

"But, Mum, he—" began Joe.

"Quiet, Joe," interrupted Mary, her voice strangled.

Ruth curled her fingers round the banister and leaned further over to better see what was happening. The wood creaked and Joe looked up. She quickly slunk back into the shadows, her heart thumping. There was a short pause and the shadows from the torch Audrey was holding danced across the walls.

"Have it your way," the man growled.

Ruth heard the slam of the front door. The scrape of a key turned in a lock.

A strange and uneasy quiet settled on the house. Even Dash had stopped barking.

"If Gordon comes to the farm again you tell me, Joe. I won't have him pestering you like this," Mary said.

"Do you not think Gordon might be wanting to help?" asked Audrey tentatively.

Ruth wondered who Gordon was. His voice had been all hard edges and angles, and he hadn't seemed very pleasant.

"We don't need his kind of help. He may use tractors and fancy machinery to run his farm, but here we do things the old way. The right way. The money from this treasure will make things better. We'll be able to pay people to work on our land," said Mary.

"Yes, of course," said Audrey, in a smaller voice than before.

Joe's feet ran lightly up the stairs. He was so swift there was no time for Ruth to return to her own bedroom. Their eyes locked and Joe's jaw clenched.

Ruth's cheeks were warm. Overhearing private conversations was becoming a bad habit of hers.

"You've no idea what you and your mum are getting yourselves into," Joe whispered. His eyes flashed like warning lamps.

"What do you mean?" Ruth whispered tightly, wondering exactly what he was warning her about.

Joe scowled.

Ruth watched him open his bedroom door and shut it quietly behind him. His words pinched uncomfortably at her insides. This would not do. He couldn't throw around comments like that and expect her to ignore them. She marched over to his door, and rapped on it, hard. There was no answer. She rapped again. Making a quick decision, she gritted her teeth, turned the door handle, and stepped inside Joe's room.

CHAPTER 12

Final Warning

Joe stood by his bed, the glow of a paraffin lamp illuminating his furrowed brow. He looked at Ruth in wide-eyed disbelief as she entered the room. She saw him quickly fold the edge of his quilt over a piece of paper lying on the bed and open his mouth to speak.

"My mum's out in *your* field in the dark and cold trying to find treasure that will help *your* family and you're being very ungrateful," said Ruth hotly, thinking it vital she got her words in first.

Joe's eyes widened further. Then he blinked. It was a long and slow blink and Ruth wondered for a horrible second if he might be about to cry. She swallowed. "I just don't understand why one minute you're nice and the next you're so…unfriendly," she said, a little more softly.

Joe looked at Ruth for a long while. The skin under his eyes was dark, like thumbprint bruises.

"You can tell me what's bothering you, Joe," Ruth said, thinking of the secret he had spoken of in the barn loft, and how he wished his dad was there to help. "If I have a problem, talking to my best friend helps. I'm not saying we're best friends or anything…or even, friends… but well, sometimes it does help to talk." Her cheeks felt warm as she waited for his response.

Joe glanced at his bed quilt, then looked up. He took a deep breath. "Close the door, will you?" he mumbled.

Ruth did as he asked then took a step closer, wondering what she was about to learn.

Joe folded back his bed cover to reveal the piece of paper again. He picked it up and held it out to Ruth.

She took it from him and held it up to the lamp. Her heart pulsed in her ears as she took in the full meaning of the words at the top of the letter.

FINAL WARNING
ROOK FARM EVICTION NOTICE

"Dad took out a loan before he died as the farm was struggling," said Joe. He deflated like a popped balloon and slumped on his bed. "Things have been worse because of bad winters this year and last. The loan hasn't been paid back for months. We'll be evicted next week if we don't pay up. The bank will own the farm, the machinery, the animals and all the land. We'll be homeless. We'll lose *everything*."

Ruth folded the letter and handed it to Joe, who lifted the edge of his mattress and placed it on top of several other pieces of paper. "But that's dreadful. Is there anything your mum can do to stop it?" she said.

"Mum doesn't know about it," admitted Joe dropping his head.

Ruth's eyebrows shot into her hairline. "What? How can she not know?"

"The bank sent other letters like this. I opened all of them and hid them. Mum was so sad after Dad died and she's been working all hours to keep the farm going. She never mentions the loan and I reckon she hoped it would just go away. I worried that if she knew about the eviction letters it would make her just give up. We must keep working on the farm and do everything we can to save it."

Ruth saw a flash of fierceness in Joe's eyes that she had also seen in Mary's eyes when talking about the farm, as if it was something to be protected at all costs. She thought of her conversation with Mary on the telephone and how she said the treasure might save the farm from ruin. "But your mum does know the farm's in trouble."

"Yes, but not how much trouble. I thought I might be able to sort this out either on my own or with my uncle Gordon's help," said Joe despondently.

"Is that the man who came to the door tonight?" asked Ruth, remembering his thin voice.

Joe nodded. "He's my dad's older brother. He lives on a farm nearby."

"Does he know about the letters from the bank?" asked Ruth.

Joe shook his head. "No. His farm is doing better than ours, but money is still short. He wouldn't be able to help even if I did tell him about the eviction."

"Isn't there any other way you could raise some money, perhaps by selling something?" asked Ruth, thinking of the objects people sometimes brought in to the museum that they'd discovered in their attics.

Joe shook his head. "You've seen how we live.

We don't own any valuables. I asked my uncle how our farm can make more money. He's been telling me to fill in some of the smaller ditches and channels to make the fields bigger and use new machinery. He even loaned us a tractor that Mum refuses to use. It just sits in the barn. She's determined we'll manage as we've always done, the way Dad ran the farm. Mum won't listen to me or my uncle. I hate all the arguing. Sometimes it feels like the war hasn't ended for us here." Joe looked utterly despairing in that moment.

"But surely it would take ages before the farm made any money from using machinery and filling in ditches. You need money to pay back the bank loan now," said Ruth.

Joe nodded. "I know."

"You've had some rotten luck, but my mum is doing her absolute best to help," Ruth said firmly.

Joe looked up. "I've nothing against you being here, it's just…" His voice trailed off as if he didn't quite know how to put his thoughts into words.

Ruth felt a flash of warmth towards him. "I think I understand a bit how you're feeling – about losing the farm I mean. We might have to move because of my parents' divorce. Leave the home I've always known.

I can't imagine living somewhere else."

Joe nodded as if he understood this perfectly well without needing to ask any further questions.

"You must tell your mum about the bank letters," Ruth carried on, a firm resolve settling within her. "Imagine what a shock it will be if you're evicted next week, and she knows nothing about it. There are still a few days for her to try and sort things out with the bank."

"I can't tell her," said Joe. He gave Ruth an anxious look. "I shouldn't have even told you."

Ruth shook her head. "Secrets like this are bad secrets and need to be shared," she said. "You should tell your mum in the morning."

Joe lowered his head. "I can't, Ruth."

Ruth felt suddenly heavy, like her trouser pockets had been filled with stones. Joe was trying to sort out his family's problems all alone, but she did not see how it was possible. The threat of losing the farm was awful and he needed to be truthful with his mum and uncle. She'd had no idea when they arrived at the farm that, as well as discovering the buried treasure, family secrets would be revealed. A feeling of dread settled over her at what might happen next.

CHAPTER 13

More to Learn

Ruth woke in dark to the sound of Dash barking downstairs. She flicked open her eyes. The room was so black she blinked and wondered whether she had opened her eyes after all. She lay still, listening to the wail of the wind outside. Shivering, she snuggled under the bedclothes, hugging the lukewarm hot-water bottle to her chest as the unfamiliar creaks and groans of the house crept through the walls. Footsteps trod lightly along the landing outside her bedroom and Ruth jolted upright at the rattle of the door handle, her heart leaping.

"It's only me. Sorry if I woke you," whispered Ruth's mum as she padded over to the bed.

"What time is it?" Ruth asked, feeling her heartbeat slow.

"A little after ten," her mum replied, as she pulled on her pyjamas.

"Did you find anything else buried in the field?" Ruth asked.

There was a pause.

"No."

"Still. If the pepper pot and ladles are treasure and the museum buys them, that will help save the farm, won't it?" said Ruth, snuggling under the covers again.

"Does the farm need saving that badly?" her mum said, slipping into bed.

"I just think things are...difficult," said Ruth, turning to face her.

"Have you been talking to Joe?" asked her mum.

"A bit," admitted Ruth.

"Poor boy. Stuck out here all alone with his mum and Audrey. He seems to carry the weight of the world on his shoulders," her mum said softly. "Remember, though, that saving the treasure and preserving a piece of history is what's important as well as the money the family may get from its sale. I think that…" She paused, breathing quietly.

"What is it, Mum?" asked Ruth.

Her mum continued to breathe quietly in the dark. She was being secretive again, and Ruth didn't like it.

"There's something peculiar about this treasure find," her mum said. "To come across one pepper pot and three ladles is very unusual. They were normally buried by the Romans in larger sets, you see. I would certainly expect to find more silver but there is nothing else to be found."

"What does that mean?" asked Ruth, pushing the hot-water bottle on to her mum's side of the bed.

"I'm saying there is more to learn about this discovery. Perhaps the other parts of the set were dug up by someone else in the past? Don't say anything to the family until I've investigated this. I don't want to cause any worry," her mum replied, reaching for Ruth's hand and giving it a light squeeze. "Maybe I missed something in the dark. I'll look again in the morning before we leave for the station. Night, darling. Sleep well."

"Night, Mum," said Ruth, rolling over to face the wall. She waited for her mum to fall asleep, but her breaths were tight and short as if her brain was still whirring. Was she thinking about who could have dug up some of the treasure already? Ruth remembered Joe's look of alarm when the treasure had been discovered and his initial unfriendliness on their arrival. Thoughts fluttered in her head. Something about the eviction notice and Joe keeping it a secret niggled at her. Then, like a match flaring, she remembered. Joe had hidden the letters from the bank under the mattress in his bedroom. She had assumed the secret she had heard him mention in the loft was about the eviction, but whatever he had been looking at up there wasn't the bank letters. Was he keeping another secret, one about the treasure, too?

Chapter 14

Eel Man

The first things Ruth heard the following morning were the thud of a door closing below the bedroom where she slept and the sound of footsteps outside. A pink pearlescent glow crept through a gap in the blackout curtains. She sat up and turned to look at her mum, who was still snoring softly. She had to be exhausted after her late-night excavations.

Yawning widely, Ruth quietly climbed out of bed, padded over to the window and pulled back the edge of one curtain. She shivered, tracing a finger over the thin film of ice clouding the inside of the glass. The bedroom overlooked the fields to the rear of the house, where a pale ghostly mist sat low on the soil. Joe was setting off across the fields. He wore a heavy black coat and woollen hat and Dash ambled alongside him as they headed towards the excavation site. It was then Ruth noticed that Joe was carrying something – a long shovel with a wide wooden handle. A horrible thought occurred to her. Joe wasn't going to dig round there himself, was he? She remembered her mum's thoughts that some of the missing treasure could have already been dug up. What was Joe up to? Pressing her nose to the icy glass, Ruth watched him cross a small wooden bridge over the ditch that led to Rook Field. He pressed on with his head low, his shoulders stooped. The mist was fast swallowing him up and soon she wouldn't be able to see him at all.

Quickly pulling on the trousers, blouse and woollen jumper she had been wearing the day before, Ruth quietly opened the door and made her way downstairs to find her coat. In the kitchen the smell of milky porridge slowly cooking on the range made her stomach rumble and she saw the breakfast table was already laid. She caught a flash of Audrey's blue coat through the window that overlooked the front yard.

Audrey carried two pails of what looked like animal feed.

Stepping out into the early morning, the chill momentarily stole Ruth's breath and she adjusted her scarf to cover her chin and lips. She set off after Joe, following his footsteps across the frost-tipped soil.

The ground was firmer than the day before and Ruth's boots crunched as she walked. Hurrying on, she soon crossed the low bridge leading to Rook Field. She paused and peered through the curling mist. Joe was kneeling, just the top of his hat visible. He was in the centre of the field, at the exact spot where the pepper pot and ladles had been found.

Ruth glanced back to the house. Should she go back and fetch her mum? There was no time. If Joe *was* meddling with the site, she needed to tell him to stop right away. She swallowed her uncertainty. But how would he react to her being there? She picked up her pace, the soles of her feet slowly numbing with cold. "Hey," she called into the mist. "Hey, Joe!"

Joe turned. Ruth was still too far away to see his expression clearly, but she was fairly certain he wasn't smiling. Dash barked gruffly, but his tail wagged. She didn't feel quite as afraid of the dog as she had when they'd first arrived. She walked on. "What are you doing?" she asked, her breath steaming in front of her.

"Nothing," said Joe lightly.

Dash sniffed around Ruth's boots as she stared at the excavation site. Stakes and twine marked out a second trench that her mum must have dug out the night before. Ruth looked at the shovel lying on the ground next to Joe. "What's that for?" she asked.

"It's a slubber – a water scoop. Terry, Audrey's fiancé, is coming to help clear some of the ditches. I was going to find the best place to start," said Joe.

Ruth crouched and placed a gloved hand on the edge of the second trench where her mum had searched and found nothing.

"I do remember what your mum said about not meddling with the site," said Joe mildly. "I would never dig here on my own."

Ruth looked up. His voice was calm and even and she felt he was telling the truth.

"Have you helped your mum on excavations before?" Joe asked.

"We went on one last summer, but I wasn't allowed to help," Ruth replied, remembering her burn of embarrassment at being told off by Mr Knight.

"You enjoyed it though?" Joe asked, tickling Dash behind the ears.

Ruth stood up and nodded. "More than I expected to. The archaeologists found some coins. It was like a proper treasure hunt. It was exciting, not knowing what might be found next."

"I can understand that," said Joe, giving Ruth a quick smile. "My dad loved looking for old things. He always hoped to find something interesting buried in the soil." His cheeks flushed and he looked away momentarily.

"Have you ever dug around the farm and looked for old things yourself?" asked Ruth lightly.

"No," said Joe quickly. Perhaps a little too quickly.

Ruth pulled her hat over her ears. Her mum had said not to mention her worries that some of the Roman treasure might have been dug up already. She needed to choose her next words carefully. "About the treasure your mum found. You didn't seem happy to show us the pepper pot when we arrived. You also didn't seem pleased when we found the ladles yesterday."

Dash whimpered at Joe's side. Joe reached down and gently pulled his dog close, as if needing the comfort.

He looked at Ruth, his eyes bright and glassy. "The pepper pot and ladles…they…" he began.

His words were interrupted by the loud *honk-honk-honk* of two snowy white swans and a few smaller wildfowl taking off from a long water-filled ditch at the far end of the field. Joe turned and stared, then set off towards the water carrying his slubber tool, Dash ambling alongside him.

Ruth hurried after them, puzzled at Joe's abrupt departure but still eager to learn what he had been about to tell her about the treasure.

"It must be the eel man," Joe said, pointing towards the water as they walked.

Ruth glanced at Joe, frustrated he hadn't answered her question. Her eyes followed his pointed finger to the ditch, only seeing a straggly wilting wall of reeds and bulrushes. But as they drew closer to the water, she heard the reeds rustle and saw a man emerge on the opposite bank. His green-and-brown clothing made him blend in with the surrounding landscape like a chameleon. Weather-worn crevices marked his face, and he carried a shotgun. A pair of brown binoculars round his neck glinted in the low sun. They swung gently from side to side as if he had just put them down. Had he been watching the excavation site? Did he know what had been found there? The thought skittered a shiver across Ruth's shoulders.

The eel man's lips twisted into a toothless grin. He gave Joe a quick nod and a wave, then slung a canvas sack over his stooped back and walked away.

"The eel man hunts and fishes round here. He lives in that hut over there in Magpie Field. It was almost falling down at one point, but my dad said if he mended it, he could live there. He eats what he kills and sells the rest at markets. Dad used to buy willow hives from him for eel-catching in the summer."

Ruth squinted and saw in the distance a small wooden building with a rusty red corrugated roof. Its chimney spat out irregular puffs of smoke. It looked more like a shack than a home, one that could easily be flattened by a gust of wind.

"I've no idea what a willow hive is but I don't like the sound of eels," said Ruth, throwing anxious glances at the water and the retreating back of the eel man. Dash was sniffing at the ditch, which flowing high, clogged with reeds and brown silt. He barked and two small black birds with vibrant red beaks gave him an indignant look and paddled away.

Joe's lips tipped into a smile. "A hive is a type of pot that you bait and put in the water. You're unlikely to see an eel though. They bury themselves in the mud at the bottom of the ditches in winter."

Ruth drew in a relieved breath. This bleak landscape with clouds as big as hills had an unnerving wildness she had never experienced before. Now the eel man had gone, she opened her mouth to ask Joe what he had been going to tell her about the pepper pot and ladles, when she heard an urgent cry.

"Joe," called a voice. "Joe!" The calls were carried high across the fields by the stillness of the morning.

Dash released a volley of barks into the air. The red-beaked birds took off on a short and laboured flight across the field.

Ruth and Joe turned. In the distance the farm looked small, like a child's playset, but a figure in a blue coat had run halfway across the fields to meet them. It was Audrey and she was waving frantically, trying to attract their attention through the rising mist. "It's your mum! Come quick, Joe!" she bellowed, cupping her hands to her mouth.

Joe and Ruth exchanged a look of alarm.

Joe dropped his slubber tool on the ground with a

thump and began to run, Dash trotting behind as he valiantly tried to keep up.

Ruth set off after them, trying to squeeze away the fear tightening her chest, wondering what they would find when they got back to the house.

CHAPTER 15

Bad to Worse

"What's happened? Is everything all right?" Ruth called, flying through the scullery door not long after Joe. Pulling off her boots and coat, she rushed into the kitchen to find her mum there with Joe and Audrey. Dash curled round Joe's legs, his tongue lolling to one side as he caught his breath.

"Terry was driving up the track when he saw Mum collapsed in Marsh Field," said Joe, pacing around the kitchen, his cheeks tight.

Ruth's mum pushed a mug of tea into Joe's hands.

Audrey twisted her fingers together. "I was feeding

the animals when Terry drove into the yard with Mary. She looked very unwell. I told him to take her to the hospital."

Joe looked grey with worry as he took a small sip of his tea.

"I hope you don't mind me using a little of your sugar ration. It will help with the shock," Ruth's mum said, gesturing at the mug. "I've made tea for you too," she said looking at Audrey and Ruth.

Audrey's bottom lip trembled, and she nodded her thanks. "I didn't realize Mary was quite so poorly. Every day she's been out in those fields before dawn. I should have stopped her," she said, nibbling on a thumbnail.

"No one can stop Mum when it comes to working on the farm. I've done my best to help," said Joe, his voice thick with despair.

"I'm sure you have helped your mum a great deal," said Ruth's mum gently. "I expect she just needs a jolly good rest."

Joe lowered his head.

Ruth picked up her tea. She hoped a rest was all that Mary needed. Her stomach fluttered with worry for Joe and his family.

Joe looked up suddenly. "Mum hasn't kept up the

health insurance payments. She said we couldn't afford to. How much will the hospital cost?"

"I don't know," admitted Audrey. She sank into a chair at the table and tilted her head to the ceiling. "Why have things gone so wrong?"

Ruth thought of their own doctor's office in London. It was somewhere her mum liked to avoid, for a visit there could be very expensive. Last Christmas she'd had a horrid ear infection which her mum tried to cure with warm compresses soaked in a solution of mustard powder. It hadn't worked, and a week later they were at the private doctors' office paying for a consultation and prescription of penicillin. Ruth's mum hadn't said anything, but Ruth knew from her mum's drawn face that this visit would mean living on powdered eggs on toast for a few weeks. This year, though, the government were bringing in a new system of free healthcare for all. "Imagine having hospitals and doctors' surgeries that you don't need to pay to visit," her mum had said with a smile after hearing a report about the new national health service on the wireless one evening. "It will make such a difference to everyone. It doesn't matter whether you are wealthy or don't have a bean. All people will be treated equally." But the system wasn't yet in place and if Mary had to stay in hospital, it would be an extra burden Joe and his family could ill afford.

"Come and sit down all of you," said Audrey. "There's nothing to be done now. We can only wait for Terry to bring news."

Ruth wished very much that the farm had a telephone. One might not be needed when things were going well, but when bad things happened… Well, she wondered how people in the past had ever managed without one.

It was an anxious and long wait for news of Mary and when Terry's van rumbled into the yard mid-morning they all ran out to greet him.

Terry's ruddy cheeks were pinched as he unfolded his stocky frame from the driver's seat and saw them all standing there. Audrey quickly made the introductions, and Ruth saw his dark eyes glinting in a friendly manner as he gently shook her hand.

"Your mum's got a chest infection," Terry said, looking at Joe. "Possibly pneumonia. The hospital's busy because of this nasty flu that's going round. He placed a hand on Joe's back. "She needs a type of medicine called antibiotics which she'll have to pay for. They said she'll get better but to expect a long recovery."

Joe looked anxious. "How long?"

Terry pressed his lips together. "They don't know. Could be…months."

Joe pushed his hair from his watery eyes, a pattern of emotions playing out across his face: relief that his mum would recover, but dismay that she would not be able to work for such a long time. "This treatment will cost a fair bit?"

Terry nodded, his dark eyes looking sorrowful. "She'll be in hospital for a few weeks at least. I'll help when I can around the farm, lad. I am sorry about this."

Ruth saw Joe glance to the stable where Storm was looking out onto the yard, his ears twitching. "What about the beet harvest? Who will help with that? The weather's about to turn as well," he said.

"We'll do everything we can to help, won't we, Terry?" said Audrey. She said the words fiercely, her hands fidgeting by her sides.

Terry nodded. "Of course."

Joe looked utterly miserable. It was an impossible situation. With the eviction looming next week, the Sternes really were on the brink of losing everything.

As Audrey, Joe and Terry walked back to the house, Ruth's mum gestured for Ruth to hang back. "I was going to excavate the site again this morning, but I don't feel happy doing that with Mary gone. I wish we could stay to help on the farm, but Mr Knight is expecting me at the museum tomorrow. I also do need to speak with him about the treasure. I think that's the best way I can help Joe and Mary right now."

"Maybe you could persuade the museum to buy the treasure quickly so they can have the money? Things are desperate," said Ruth, folding her arms round her middle to stop herself from shivering in the cold.

"Well, I'm not sure about that," said her mum with a frown. She looked like she wanted to say more, but instead clamped her lips shut as if she had already said too much. Ruth knew better than to question her mum further. Now was not the time.

As Ruth half listened to her mum chat quietly about train times and walking down the track to get the bus to Ely station, the urge to help Joe out of this predicament grew inside her like a seed being watered. He was facing the loss of his home, just like she was – and she was the only one who knew the secret he was keeping about the eviction. As a result, the words popped out of her mouth almost taking her by surprise. "I want to stay here on the farm to help, while you go back to London, Mum."

Ruth's mum's eyebrows arched upwards. "What?"

"Please, Mum. There's so much to do on the farm. You heard what Joe said about needing to get the harvest in and the weather changing," said Ruth.

"No, Ruth. I'm not leaving you here," her mum replied.

Ruth pushed her shoulders back. "You cycled all over London delivering urgent documents during the war. You helped where it was needed. Joe and Audrey need my help now," she pleaded. "Think of my friends who were evacuated for months and months. This would only be for a couple of days, just until the end of the week. We've nothing planned for the rest of the school holidays. I'll be much more use here than at home."

Ruth's mum tilted her head; she seemed to be thinking. "But how could I let you stay here without Mary's blessing?" she said at last.

"Wouldn't Mary want what is best for the farm?" asked Ruth. "She's ill, Mum. She needs help."

Ruth's mum looked over at the house and bit on her lower lip. She sighed, took Ruth's hands and squeezed them. "You are a thoughtful girl. I'm sure Joe and Audrey would welcome another pair of hands. They seem a nice family and Audrey is very responsible. Are you really happy to do this?"

"Yes, I am," said Ruth firmly.

"Let me put it to Audrey and see what she says then," said her mum.

Ruth squeezed her mum's fingers in gratitude, while also feeling an edge of guilt. She badly wanted to help Joe, but staying at the farm would also allow her to find out more about the treasure. That was the only way she would be able to help her mum and their own situation. It was more important than ever that she learned the truth.

CHAPTER 16

Back to London

"Mum was going to finish collecting the beets in Marsh Field today. I need to get the job done before the weather turns," said Joe, over a subdued late breakfast of thick bacon and yolky eggs that Audrey had insisted on preparing. She had gladly agreed to Ruth's offer to stay at the farm for the rest of the week, enveloping her in a quick and grateful hug.

"Good lad," said Terry. "There's nothing to be gained by sitting around and moping. Later I'll take the things Audrey's collected for your mum over to the hospital. They won't allow visitors, but I'll telephone from my own mum's house each day for an update."

Joe smiled his thanks.

"In the meantime, I'll get on and clear the ditches in Gull Field. The threat of flooding was bad there last time I looked. You can't afford to lose that field of beet," continued Terry, as he munched on a slice of toast. Terry was a jolly chap and Ruth felt buoyed up by his positive attitude.

"I'll get the tools ready," said Audrey, tightening the belt of her dungarees. "I'll do anything I can to help."

"Me too," said Ruth, glancing to the door. Her mum had gone upstairs to pack her things.

Terry gave them both a look filled with gratitude and clapped his hands. "Teamwork. That's the spirit."

Ruth tried to imprint the rainbow burst of flavours in her memory as she finished her breakfast. The small eggs her mum brought home in exchange for ration coupons seemed to be from a different species of bird entirely. "Did you cook for your family when you lived in Norwich?" she asked Audrey, wishing she and her mum could breakfast like this in London every day.

Audrey looked up. "Yes. My sister, Emma, loves my cakes most of all. She has a very sweet tooth."

"Have they ever been to visit you here?" asked Ruth.

Audrey shook her head and began to stack the empty plates.

"I hope I get to meet your sister and the rest of your family one day," said Terry, wiping his lips with a frayed napkin. "I sometimes wonder if Audrey is keeping me away from them for a reason."

"No, it's not like that," said Audrey, flushing. "There's just always so much to do here and my family are so busy too."

Terry reached into the pocket of his coat, which was hanging on the back of his chair. He pulled out a paper bag and passed it to Audrey.

"What's this?" she asked, looking bemused.

"Go on, open it," urged Terry. He was looking very pleased with himself.

Audrey unfolded the top of the bag and pulled out a bottle of perfume. Her eyebrows tugged together. "You didn't need to buy me this."

"I wanted to," said Terry, grinning. "I like spoiling you."

"You should save your money. You keep telling us you're short," said Joe, in the gentle way you might scold a brother.

Terry looked at Joe silently for a few seconds. "That's

true, but I can still afford to buy the odd present."

Audrey got up and gave Terry a quick peck on the cheek. "Thank you. But please don't spend your money on me. I've got all I need."

Ruth heard her mum's feet on the stairs. She walked into the kitchen carrying the small suitcase, having told Ruth she would collect the heavy rucksack of tools when she returned, later in the week. She glanced at her watch. "I really should be getting to the train station."

"I can give you a lift. It's not far," offered Terry.

"Oh, thank you, that would be a help," Ruth's mum replied. "Before I go, I do have a request. Would you mind terribly if I took a ladle to show Mr Knight at the museum?"

"No, you can't take anything," said Joe, his voice dropping like a stone into a well.

Ruth frowned.

"I understand you want to keep it safe, Joe. I do too. But the museum can help value it and that will help the farm," said Ruth's mum.

Joe shook his head. "The treasure can't leave the farm."

"Why not?" asked Ruth, unable to sit silently and ignore Joe's strange behaviour.

"It's…what my dad would have wanted," Joe said. His eyes flickered to the dresser and the objects his dad had found in the fields.

Ruth's frown deepened, thinking back to Joe's whispers about his secret in the barn and wishing his dad was there to make things right. Could Joe's dad have been involved in digging up the missing parts of the treasure set?

Terry gave Joe a gentle look. "Your dad would want what's best for the farm, lad. Let Harriett take a ladle to London."

Joe threw Terry an unhappy look, then sighed and nodded.

Ruth's mum smiled. "I promise I'll look after it, Joe. I'll carry it carefully and bring it back on Saturday when I come to collect Ruth. I'll also wrap up the remaining ladles with the pepper pot and put them all in the dresser cupboard. They'll be safe in there."

Ruth said goodbye to her mum as Terry turned his van round in the yard ready to head for the train station. Gladly accepting the money her mum pressed into her palm for emergencies, she waved vigorously as the van bumped down the long farm track. Ruth watched and listened until it was out of sight and the rumble of its engine could be heard no more. Audrey was assembling the ditch-clearing tools at the back of the house. Joe had taken Storm and the cart to collect beets in Marsh Field. He was expecting Ruth to join him after she had said goodbye to her mum. But for the time being Ruth found herself unexpectedly alone. A glint of sun on a puddle in front of the big barn directed her gaze. Her fingers tingled in anticipation. Pulling the front door to the farmhouse closed, she rubbed her arms against the cold and headed across the yard to the barn, determined to take this opportunity to find out what secrets Joe was hiding up in the loft.

CHAPTER 17

Old Things

Ruth drew in a quiet breath as she stood looking up at the barn loft. She climbed the ladder steadily and, peeping over the top rung, she blinked in surprise. Piles of abandoned farm tools – forks with missing spikes, slubbers without handles, a huddle of hedgehog-like rectangular broom bristles and stacks of rusting buckets – littered the space. It wasn't these items that surprised her, however, it was the objects lined up on a wooden shelf that ran the length of the barn.

Clambering into the loft, Ruth wound her way past the farm implements to the shelf. She gingerly picked up a child's brown leather shoe, the laces still tightly pulled. The leather was tough and crinkly, as if it had been submerged in water. Next to it was a small handwritten card. She swiped away the dust with a forefinger. *Found in Gull Field, January 1929.*

Placing it down she picked up a mug without a handle. The cream china glaze was mottled, like cracked ice. *Found in Marsh Field, November 1932.* She moved from object to object, examined weathered pieces of green glass with rounded corners, a pile of mismatched blue and white china, a tarnished cutlery fork with a missing prong and a peculiar stone with a jagged hole in its centre. A handwritten card accompanied each object. These looked like more of the items that Joe's dad had dug up in his fields over the years, a museum of oddities that must be full to the brim of memories for Joe and his family.

In the far-right corner of the loft was an old green sofa. The seat cushions sagged with the imprints of the people who had sat on it. Ruth saw the floorboards were scuffed there, less dusty than in other parts of the loft. Perhaps Joe came up here often to sit among his dad's old things and remember happier times.

Ruth's breath steamed in the cold and her teeth

began to chatter. She looked around the loft for anything that could have made the clunking sound when she'd overheard Joe whispering about his secret the previous day. It had sounded like the lid of a box closing...

She looked again at the chair. There was quite a gap between the sagging seat cushion and the wooden floor. She quickly walked over, kneeled, and pushed a hand underneath. Her fingers felt something solid and crumbly. She pulled out a hardened bread crust and threw it over the back of the sofa in disgust. Slipping her hand under the chair again, this time she felt something small and cold. Her fingers curled round the tiny object, and she pulled it out. It was a small silver heart charm engraved with the letter E. Could it belong on Audrey's bracelet? Ruth pushed it into her trouser pocket.

Wiping her hands on her trousers, she stood up and looked around the loft again. Her eyes settled on the dusty floor and the scuffed footprints by the chair, an idea occurring to her. Joe's footprints would provide a clue to his movements up here. Ruth began to wind her way back through the old farm implements, her eyes glued to the floorboards. She walked past a huddle of broom heads and a rusty bucket with an eye-like hole in one side. Then she paused. To the right of the bucket were some shovels stacked against the wall. The area near them was scuffed, just as it was by the chair. Someone visited this part of the loft quite regularly.

Bending down, she looked into the gap behind the shovels and saw something lurking. A rusting, blue metal toolbox. Pleased with her detective skills, Ruth carefully pulled the box from its hiding place and opened the hinged lid. It was full of hammers, screwdrivers and smaller boxes of nails and screws. But it was hidden out of sight, which meant it must contain something interesting.

Ruth took out the tools one by one, laying them on the floor beside her. Then, at the very bottom of the box she saw a hessian-wrapped bundle. It was slim, a little longer than her hand and rested on a yellowing envelope. She remembered that the pepper pot had been wrapped in hessian too, when they'd arrived. Ruth's breaths quickened.

Her fingers were numb with cold as she lifted out both the object and the envelope. Slowly peeling back the cloth, guilt gnawed at Ruth all the while. She shouldn't be up here rooting around, but her curiosity to find out what Joe was hiding was too strong to ignore. The worries her mum had about the Roman ladles and pepper pot being part of a larger set were spinning through Ruth's head. She imagined Mr Knight's eyes widening in surprise to hear that Ruth – a child no less – had solved that mystery. Drawing back the final fold, she gasped at the sight before her. A small and rounded piece of metal that looked like a spearhead and fitted in the palm of her hand, plus four azure-blue marbles, their surfaces pitted and scratched. She peered at the spearhead. The metal was dull and brown. It was shaped like a javelin, with a blunt end and a socket for binding it to a handle.

Ruth gingerly picked up one of the marbles and examined it. It was smaller than a coin, perfectly smooth and had a hole in its centre. She frowned. This wasn't a marble, it was a bead.

A thrill made the hairs on Ruth's arms stand on end. The items were old, she was certain of it. She had a vague memory of seeing similar beads and spearheads in the museum, but however hard she racked her brains she could not remember how old they were. But the items didn't look as if they belonged to the same set of silver tableware as the Roman ladles and pepper pot.

Ruth glanced at the shelf of odd things discovered on the farm and the small notes saying when and where they had been found. Why weren't the spearhead and beads on display? They weren't obviously valuable or made of precious metal, so she couldn't see a need for them to be hidden like this. She glanced at the envelope. Perhaps the answer to that question lay inside. It was addressed to Mr Sterne at Rook Farm – Joe's Dad.

Rooks cawed on the barn's roof, as the envelope sat as lightly as one of the birds' feathers in Ruth's lap. It felt uncomfortable to be thinking about reading a letter addressed to Joe's dad, but what if the contents provided the answers to some of the mysteries that were looming? Unable to resist the temptation, she quickly slipped out the sheet of crinkled paper and read the letter. Ruth rubbed her eyes and read it again, and then for a third time. She sat back on her heels and puffed out a breath. Joe did have a secret – and it was one she never could have guessed.

CHAPTER 18

Thicket

Ruth needed to talk to Joe at once, for what she'd learned from the letter didn't only affect his family, but hers too. Carefully wrapping up the spearhead and beads, she placed them back in the toolbox and returned them to their hiding place. She kept the letter, however, gently pushing it into her coat pocket.

Making her way to the loft opening she was about to clamber down the ladder when she heard the rumble of a van pulling into the yard. Had Terry returned from the station already? Time had slipped by unnoticed. Ruth listened quietly. A door slammed shut. Then the clunk of another door opening and closing. Footsteps crossed the yard. The same footsteps thumped into the barn below. Ruth held her breath. She'd stayed at the farm to help, so to be caught snooping up here would not be good at all.

Ruth peered over the edge of the loft opening and saw Terry stride into the barn carrying two metal containers. She could hear liquid sloshing inside them as he walked.

Terry placed the containers on the ground and unscrewed the cap of the larger one. He picked up a stick leaning against the barn wall and gave the contents a stir. He sniffed.

Ruth wrinkled her nose as the unmistakable smell of petrol wafted up through the rafters. Terry gave the containers a slightly regretful look, screwed the cap back on and carried them to the rear of the barn. Ruth watched silently as he hid them under a sheet of canvas behind the tractor, placing several broken wicker baskets on top that were filled with small forks and trowels. His actions were strange. What was he doing? Standing back, Terry wiped his hands on his overalls and puffed out a breath. Turning on his heel he left the barn, his feet thumping across the yard.

Waiting a few minutes more to be sure he had gone, Ruth scrambled down the ladder, out of the barn and into the day. The low sunlight was blinding after the gloom of the dusty loft and she blinked, dots swimming before her eyes. She would fetch her coat straight away and then go and find Joe.

Ruth dodged half-frozen puddles as she strode across the yard and through the farm gate towards Marsh Field, where Joe was working. This time she had no trouble with the catch. She felt for the envelope in her pocket and suffered a twinge of anxiety about what Joe would say when he found out she knew his secret.

Continuing alongside a water-filled ditch, she eventually reached a small bridge leading to the field to her left. The air was crisp and her boots trampled over the light frost. In the distance she saw Joe with Storm and the cart. She hurried along, passing one of the few thickets of trees she had seen on the farm. It was novel to be surrounded by bare twisted branches and mulchy leaf litter after so much soil and flatness. She was so absorbed in looking at the thicket that she stumbled across the two men talking without any warning at all.

"Are you sure this is right?" said one man to the other in a voice that sounded like gravel in a tin can. He had his cap pulled low over his face, and was holding a gun. It was the eel man.

"It's what needs to be done," said an arrow-nosed man in a green coat and black wellington boots. His thin voice was familiar too. It was Gordon Sterne, Joe's uncle.

Ruth ducked into the gloom of the trees. She had overheard Mary tell him to stay off her land. What was he doing here?

"She'll be furious if she finds out it was us," said the eel man, his voice uncertain. He adjusted the binoculars that hung round his neck.

"She won't find out if we're careful," replied Gordon.

There was a short pause. "All right then," the eel man agreed, but Ruth sensed he was reluctant to do what he had been asked.

"Keep it between us. No one must know," said Gordon tightly.

The eel man tipped his cap in acknowledgment.

Giving a brief nod, Gordon set off across the fields.

The eel man looked after him for a second or two, deep in thought. He turned to the thicket and pulled a green packet of woodbines from his pocket. Ruth heard the strike of a match, saw a flare of orange as he lit a cigarette.

Leaf litter rustled under Ruth's boots as she turned to leave. Her insides quivered as she saw the eel man swing the gun under his arm and step forward, his boots cracking over the twig-strewn ground. Ruth held herself as still as the gnarled tree trunk she was lurking by, as the strong smell of cigarette smoke wafted round the trees.

There was a sudden noise from above and rooks cawed and bustled into the air like black handkerchiefs.

The eel man looked up sharply, his cigarette clamped between his bared, yellowing teeth. He raised his gun to the sky.

He didn't know she was there. What if he misfired? "Stop!" The words fell from Ruth's lips and the birds scattered and disappeared.

The eel man lowered his gun. "Who's hiding in there?"

Ruth's legs felt jelly-like. There was little point in hiding or running. She strode forward, trying to feel brave.

The creases in the eel man's face deepened. "You're the girl I saw with Joe yesterday, by the ditch."

Ruth nodded.

"What are you doing in the trees?"

"I'm…on my way to help Joe," said Ruth, a chill throbbing through her bones.

"He's in the field over there," said the eel man, pointing to where Joe was working. "You and that lady were out in the fields digging yesterday. Did you find something?" he asked suddenly.

The sun glimmered on his binoculars. The circles of glass seemed to stare at Ruth like another pair of enquiring eyes. "I'd better go. Joe's expecting me to help with the beet harvest," she said, wanting to get away.

The eel man gave her a slow and thoughtful nod, tipped his cap and strode off in the same direction as Joe's uncle, his gun hoisted over his shoulder as if he were marching into battle.

Ruth pressed on, the razor-sharp light making her eyes water. She thought of the eel man's swinging binoculars. He had been watching them while they had dug the excavation trenches in Rook Field. He had admitted as much by asking if they'd found something. The land was flat and open here, but the ditches and watercourses still provided good hiding places. It made her feel odd and a little exposed.

When Joe saw Ruth approaching, he stood up, a turnip-like vegetable limp in each hand. The beets were scattered all over the ground, like a storm of giant hailstones had landed on the field. Ruth felt the edge of the envelope in her pocket, her thoughts about the eel man and his conversation with Joe's uncle quickly replaced with the anxiety of confronting Joe with what she knew.

Breath steamed from Storm's velvety nose as he stood patiently with the cart, while Dash sniffed around the beets as if hoping one of them might miraculously turn into a tasty bone. He wagged his tail and barked.

Ruth smiled. She was becoming used to his gruff greetings.

"It's tiring work," said Joe, giving Ruth a grimace. "Thanks for offering to help." He turned and hurled the beets into the cart. Storm dipped his head and snorted, as if asking Joe to hurry up.

"Um. Yes. I will help, but there's something I need to talk to you about first," Ruth said.

Joe looked at her expectantly.

Ruth felt as if her ribs were squeezing together, making it difficult to catch her breath. This was harder than she thought. She pulled the envelope out. "I found this. In the barn loft with the spearhead and glass beads."

Joe's eyes became as wide as full moons. "What…? How…?" he spluttered, dropping the beets he was holding and almost tripping in his hurry to reach her.

Ruth felt a sway of guilt. "I'm sorry I snooped, but I heard you in the barn yesterday. You mentioned having a secret. I thought it might be to do with the treasure." She paused and swallowed the dryness in her mouth. "You lied about the treasure, Joe. You've been lying to us all."

Joe shook his head miserably. His eyes were suddenly watery, and he rubbed them roughly on his coat sleeve.

"My mum's gone to London believing the Romans buried the ladles and pepper pot on your land centuries ago. But the treasure wasn't even from your land," continued Ruth.

The rooks cawed, fussed and settled in the thicket of trees, the only sound for miles around.

Joe was so still and so quiet, Ruth's stomach clenched in unease. "This affects my mum as well as your family, but I don't fully understand what this letter means. Please tell me everything and don't leave a thing out," she urged, taking the letter from the envelope and looking at it again.

Joe nodded and bowed his head, his lips trembling. "I don't know if I can. People will be hurt by the secrets I've been keeping, including you and your mum. I'm sorry, Ruth. I really am."

CHAPTER 19

Mr Hartest

Ruth stood quietly, her body fizzing with concern as she looked again at the letter she had found hidden in the barn loft.

73 Belvoir Street,
Norwich
Tel. Norwich 3460

25 May 1942,

Dear Mr Sterne,
Please accept this letter as confirmation that I have

passed to you several items of Roman treasure, a silver pepper pot and three ladles, for safekeeping at Rook Farm. As agreed, you shall bury the objects at a location on the farm known only to the two of us. I greatly appreciate your assistance in helping me to hide these items and in return I promise to help you excavate the site at which you found the spearhead and glass beads, which I suspect could be very old.

I have recorded the location of the spearhead and beads in my field notebook and remain very much convinced they signify that a bigger discovery could be made at your farm. However, I would urge you not to disturb the site where you found them and to wait for my return and assistance. This will ensure anything buried is kept safe and damage avoided.

You have been a good friend to me, Mr Sterne, and I appreciate your help in this delicate matter. I feel, in this time of war, valuable objects are safer buried in the ground than kept in a museum. I look forward to meeting you again during more peaceful times.

Yours truly,
Colin Hartest

Joe cleared his throat and began to speak slowly and softly as Dash snaked round his legs. "Mr Hartest visited all the farms near these parts while I was small. He had a passion for old things; worked at a museum, I think. He and Dad struck up a close friendship; they had much in common, including a love of the past and wanting to look after any objects that they found." Joe reached down and fondled Dash's ears. "I was dozing in the barn loft one afternoon. I was seven and would often hide from Dad when there was hard work to be done. I heard Dad and Mr Hartest talking down below. I spied on them. I saw Dad show him the glass beads and spearhead. Mr Hartest's face turned as purple as a beetroot. He thought they could be very old and got excited." Joe paused, his eyes unfocused and far away.

"What happened next?" asked Ruth, the wind whipping her hair around her face.

Joe looked up. "Mr Hartest offered to help Dad excavate the site where he'd found the beads and spearhead, but said it should wait until after the war. He said we might be invaded by Germans and how bad it would be if we found something valuable and it fell into the wrong hands. Then he and Dad left the barn and I heard no more."

Ruth frowned. "So the whole reason for burying the treasure on your land was to keep it safe during the war?"

Joe nodded. "Mr Hartest returned a few days later, in the evening; Mum was already in bed. I was watching from the kitchen window. Mr Hartest passed Dad a canvas bag. He made some notes in a little book, shook Dad's hand and left. Later that night from my bedroom I saw Dad with a shovel and a flashlight heading for the fields. It was supposed to be blackout and I was scared Dad was breaking the rules. I went to see him."

Ruth's brain rushed to piece together what happened next. "The pepper pot and ladles were in the bag and your dad buried them in Rook Field – the place your mum found them?"

"Yes," said Joe. "Dad dug a hole. He took the items out of the bag and put them in the hole, then covered them with soil."

Ruth thought about what Mr Hartest had said in his letter. "Why did Mr Hartest choose to bury these items here? Why not somewhere else? And why didn't he do it himself?"

Joe shrugged. "Our farm is isolated. Dad and Mr Hartest also liked and trusted one another. If some of the other farmers round here found something valuable in the ground, they would have sold it on to private collectors for the highest price. Dad and Mr Hartest weren't like that. They appreciated the objects for what they were."

Ruth thought of the dresser in the kitchen and the shelf in the loft displaying Joe's dad's finds. She imagined he and her mum would have had much in common and felt a renewed sadness for Joe that his dad was no longer around. "What did your dad say that night in the field?" asked Ruth.

Joe frowned. "He made me swear to tell no one about the treasure, not even Mum. He didn't even tell his brother – my uncle Gordon. Dad even destroyed the canvas bag Mr Hartest had brought the treasure in. He said it was safer the objects were just covered in soil, so if someone did find them it would look less suspicious."

"Do you know where Mr Hartest got the objects in the first place?" asked Ruth.

"No. Dad never mentioned it, although I've also wondered about that," said Joe.

"And you've kept this a secret from everyone for all this time?" said Ruth, shaking her head at the lengths Mr Hartest and Joe's dad had gone to.

Joe nodded. His chin wobbled.

"But after your dad died, couldn't you have told your mum?" asked Ruth.

Joe puffed out a breath and kicked at a nearby beet, which rolled into a rut. Dash yapped and ambled after it. "Mum doesn't have the same love of the past as my dad – you've seen how set she is on selling the ladles and pepper pot to the museum. My dad hadn't been feeling well last summer. One day he took me up to the barn loft and showed me the glass beads, spearhead and the letter from Mr Hartest in the toolbox. And he said if anything ever happened to him, I would need to find Mr Hartest to give him his treasure back. Before Dad got round to telling me where the things were buried, he died."

"I'm so sorry, Joe," said Ruth, feeling his weight of responsibility keenly. "But it's been almost six years since Mr Hartest wrote that letter. Didn't your dad wonder why he hadn't come back?"

Joe nodded. "I asked my dad about that. He'd written and telephoned Mr Hartest, but got no reply. He was still hoping he would just turn up at the farm one day. After Dad died, I went to the telephone box every day for two weeks and tried to get through to

Mr Hartest, but no one ever answered. I sent a letter but got no reply. I think something might have happened to him during the war. Maybe my dad thought that too but didn't want to accept it."

"Oh, Joe." Ruth realized with the force of a storm what a predicament he was in. The rooks seemed to agree, as they cawed and chattered in the trees.

"I couldn't believe my eyes when Mum ploughed up the pepper pot. I suppose Dad hadn't buried the treasure as deeply as he should have done. She thought the treasure would solve all of the farm's money worries. Then your mum arrived from the museum and…I just couldn't tell anyone the truth. The ladles and pepper pot belong to Mr Hartest. We can't sell them to help save the farm."

Poor Joe. He had been keeping so many secrets from his mum. No wonder he'd seemed so angry when she had first arrived; he was all knotted up inside. "Were the ladles and pepper pot the only things your dad buried for Mr Hartest?" asked Ruth, thinking of her mum's fruitless search for the other parts of the treasure set.

Joe nodded. "As far as I know."

Ruth straightened her gloves. "My mum thinks the

treasure set is incomplete and some of it could have been dug up already."

Joe's eyes widened. "Is that why she was out digging late last night?"

"I reckon so," said Ruth. She had been hoping to discover what had happened to the missing parts of the treasure set in the barn loft, but instead she'd uncovered another secret. What would her mum and Mr Knight say when they discovered that the Roman treasure did not come from Rook Farm? She felt a wave of heat at the thought of having to explain everything to her mum and Mr Knight. He already thought her hopeless and this would just emphasize his belief. It could also be hugely embarrassing for her mum.

An idea was nudging at the edges of Ruth's brain as she stared at the beets scattered across the soil. "The spearhead and beads *were* found on your farm, Joe. In the letter Mr Hartest seems confident there may be more things like it to be found here."

Joe looked up. "I've already thought about that. But we'll never know where to look unless we find Mr Hartest and his notebook."

"Are you sure your dad didn't make a note of where he found them?" Ruth asked.

Joe nodded. "I searched through all his papers. I found nothing."

With a burst of clarity Ruth suddenly understood what they needed to do next. "Firstly, we need to straighten out what happened with the ladles and pepper pot – and where these are from. Then we need to do everything we can to find Mr Hartest and his notebook. Mr Knight might send someone to excavate if we knew where the beads and spearhead had been found."

"Do you think that's possible?" asked Joe. His voice was rimmed with a hope that Ruth hadn't heard since they arrived. Ruth was filled with fresh hope too. They had something that was feeling like a plan, which could solve both of their problems, and while she hadn't worked out the full details, she realized then she didn't have to. Joe was there and they would work this out. Together.

CHAPTER 20

Emma

Ruth helped Joe in Marsh Field for the remainder of the day, finding a soothing rhythm in hurling beets into the cart, which Storm pulled steadily up and down the field. Mid-afternoon they stopped work and tucked in to thickly cut slices of bread and butter, wedges of creamy cheese and tangy pickles, all washed down with warm tea from Joe's flask. She and Joe had spoken at length about the glass beads and spearhead, Joe running through possible places his dad might have found them. But the farm was vast and with no clues to the location of the discovery it was an impossible task

– they could hardly dig up every field, especially as many of them were in use. Finding Mr Hartest's notebook was the only way of learning where the objects had been found.

It was nearing dusk as they walked back up the farm track with Storm and the cart, and the sky above their heads suddenly filled with a whooshing sound. Ruth looked up to see a mass of tiny black dots moving like a shoal of fish across the darkening sky. The birds swooped and wheeled then dropped like a rock. "What is that?" she asked in amazement.

"Starlings," said Joe, his head tipped to the sky too. "We often see them in winter. My dad said they stick together like this to avoid predators on the way to roost."

The patterns and swirls the birds made were like a pulsing heart. These birds, the way the sun moved across the sky, the way clouds formed and dispersed and the way the field had slowly emptied of the beets they had collected were all a constant reminder that life was moving onward with no means of pause or delay. It should have been an unsettling thought, but Ruth found to her surprise it was strangely comforting.

They arrived back at the farm to find Audrey tending

to the vegetable plot. Her hair was pulled back with a bright blue scarf and her cheeks were mottled pink. She flew from one task to another in a dizzying rush, like a bee collecting pollen.

Joe unbridled Storm in the yard and led him to a water trough. His tail swished as he dipped his nose and drank deeply.

"You look chilled to the bone. Go in and warm up," said Audrey, leaning on her fork to catch her breath.

"I'll help Joe with Storm first," said Ruth.

"Thank you," Audrey said wearily. "Terry and I cleared out sections of ditches in danger of breaching their banks. There's more to be done though. He's round the back of the barn cleaning and sharpening the tools."

As Audrey adjusted her hand on the fork, Ruth caught a glimpse of her bracelet. She suddenly remembered the charm she had found in the barn loft earlier that day. "I found this," she said, pulling it from her pocket and holding it out in her palm. "I thought it might be yours."

Audrey stilled. "Oh. It is. I thought I'd lost it." Her voice was whispered and low. She stuck the fork on the ground and took the charm.

"It's a pretty bracelet. What is the E for?" Ruth asked.

Audrey's fingers curled round it. "Emma. My sister."

"That's lovely," said Ruth. She'd often hoped for a brother or sister, someone to play with as she grew up. She felt a sudden burst of envy for Audrey's charm bracelet and all it represented. "Will you tell me about the other charms and what they mean?" she asked shyly.

Audrey glanced at the bracelet and seemed to be thinking about Ruth's question. She held out her wrist. "Well, you see this little dancing shoe. My dad…he makes shoes just like it in a factory in Norwich. And see this shell? It came from a seaside trinket shop in Cromer. The four of us went for the day. It was boiling hot. Our shoulders got sunburned." Audrey's eyes were bright with the memories. Then her face dropped. She pulled down her right coat sleeve until the bracelet was hidden.

"Your family must be proud of you helping Mary and Joe run the farm," said Ruth.

Audrey frowned. "Proud," she said slowly, as if the word was foreign and unfamiliar. She shook her head, as if trying to rid herself of a troubling thought. She looked at Ruth and smiled, but the skin by her eyes didn't crinkle. "You help Joe with Storm, and I'll see you later. I'm cooking tea for Terry's mum at her house but will be back by nine o'clock. I'll leave a pie for you and Joe in the range."

In the stables Joe showed Ruth how to fill Storm's rack with oats and chopped straw. The straw made Ruth sneeze, which caused Storm to swing his head, making Joe smile. She had learned that afternoon that a horse could be large but also gentle and Ruth found she wasn't at all afraid, enjoying the warm fug in the air. As they worked, they talked again about the notebook and how they might find it and Mr Hartest.

"I think the only thing to do is to visit Mr Hartest's house in Norwich," said Ruth. "Even if he isn't there, a neighbour might know something."

Joe's face dropped, as he brushed Storm's thick, black mane. "But I can't leave the farm and go to Norwich. There's too much to do. I can't let Mum down. And we've no money for the bus fares."

Ruth placed a hand on Storm's flank and his warmth seeped through her damp glove. "My mum left me some emergency money. This is an emergency, Joe, for both of us. If we find the location of real buried treasure on your farm it might be worth something, which could help save the farm. It would also make Mr Knight happy and could help my mum get the job at the museum, which means I get to keep my home too." The horse flicked his velvet ears. Ruth swallowed a burn at the base of her throat, thinking of the mural on her bedroom wall. The December before last, when her mum and dad were still together, she'd arrived home from a walk to find her dad adding a small Christmas tree to the mural. Bright blobs of silver paint made the miniature decorations shine like the brightest stars in the sky. She'd hurled her arms round her dad's neck and planted a kiss on his cheek.

He had grinned. "We don't have much money for presents, but I hoped this would be something special you'd be able to enjoy for years to come."

Ruth leaned her head against Storm's flank now and closed her eyes, feeling the steady thrum of his heartbeat as she thought of leaving the painted Christmas tree behind. The memories of home were so vivid she had a sudden, sharp longing to be back in her bedroom, pressing her hands to the mural and absorbing all the images her dad had painted so she would never forget. She knew the potential loss of her own home was not as bad as Joe losing the farm, but it still stung. "We have to find the notebook, Joe. It's the only way to try and make things right."

CHAPTER 21

Watched

Thick fog was stealing across the dark yard as Ruth and Joe left the stables. Audrey and Terry had already gone to have tea at his mum's house and while Joe went to feed the cows in the shed, Ruth returned to the house. Dash announced her arrival with a series of gruff barks.

Checking her watch, Ruth saw it was almost six o'clock, and she quickly switched on the electric lights. Thankfully there was no cut in supply. She blinked at the sight of the scullery sink piled high with dirty pots and pans and the blobs of uncooked pastry scattered around the kitchen table like tiny hills. Audrey struck her as a tidy person, who didn't like mess. Mary being in hospital and worries over the farm must be playing deeply on her mind.

As Ruth wiped the table and washed the pans, she thought all the while about Mr Hartest's field notebook. Her mum would return to collect her on Saturday – a little over two days' time. Could they find Mr Hartest and his notebook by then? Still pondering this, she looked around the kitchen for other ways she might help Audrey, liking the grown-up sense of satisfaction straightening the house gave her. Noticing a wicker linen basket of folded laundry, she carried it upstairs. Three of Audrey's blouses lay on top of the basket, the collars and sleeves pressed as sharply as folded paper.

The earlier wind outside had dropped, and the house was cold and stiff with silence. Ruth paused at the top of the stairs, hearing a noise. Her breath suddenly quickened at being alone. Hurrying along the landing Ruth saw Audrey's bedroom door was slightly ajar. Deciding to quickly leave the laundry on Audrey's bed and return to the kitchen and Dash, she pushed the door open and stepped inside.

Flicking on the light switch, she saw the room was

neat and tidy. A framed watercolour of fenland fields hung on the wall opposite the bed. The sky in the painting was the palest blue and dotted with birds; the fields were a dusky yellow. The fens must be an entirely different place in the summer and Ruth had a sudden longing to return when the sun shone golden and the days were long. Placing the linen basket down, she laid Audrey's blouses on top of the pink bed quilt.

Ruth picked up the basket and turned to leave, but as she swung round, she accidentally nudged the small dressing table that stood by the bed. There was a rustle as something fell to the floor. Placing the basket down again, Ruth's eyes were drawn to the curious object that had fallen onto the carpet. It was a small swan, made from woven strands of straw. The swan's neck was tightly braided, and its feathered tail splayed behind it elegantly. Perhaps it had been another present from Terry? She picked it up and placed it next to the spot it had most likely fallen from, between a bottle of perfume and an ashtray with four silver-heart charms nestled at the centre. Ruth saw with surprise the silver letter E she had returned to Audrey earlier that day. Beside it were two letter Ms and the letter A. *Emma*. Ruth frowned. Why weren't these charms on Audrey's bracelet? She spent much of her time caring for other families but did not see much of her own. Throwing the charms one last confused glance, Ruth picked up the linen basket and left the room.

Dash stuck to Ruth's side in the kitchen as she waited for Joe. Kneeling by the dog's rug, Ruth tentatively stroked his silky head and ears. His tail thumped and he licked his lips, then her nose. She giggled, wiping her wet nose on her sleeve. Ruth thought of Mrs Drake and her fluffy white cat. Perhaps she and her mum could get a pet when they returned home. The thought that they would do new things together that her dad would miss out on made pockets of sadness bubble up inside her. He would be so interested to hear about the treasure discovery. If he had still been living at home, they could all have chatted about it over tea.

She glanced at the dresser cupboard where the treasure was hidden, suddenly wanting a longer look at the discovery so she could imprint the details on her mind and tell her dad about it herself. Taking the hessian bundle from the cupboard, Ruth sat at the kitchen table. Carefully unwrapping the empress pepper pot and two ladles, she examined them, letting her fingers roam over the bumps and folds of the ancient metal, marvelling that they could have been made over one thousand years ago.

The range pipes ticked and creaked. Dash suddenly growled, bared his teeth and ran to the hallway, his nails clicking on the floor tiles. Ruth looked up, the skin on her shoulders prickling. She had a sudden sensation of being watched. The window was a rectangle of black and wisps of fog grasped at the glass. Sitting quietly for a second or two, Ruth stilled her breathing, her fingers still clasped round the pepper pot. She shook herself mentally. There was no need to be afraid. Joe was outside and sure to return from finishing his tasks soon.

Dash snarled and Ruth heard his claws scratch and scrape at the front door. *Was* someone there? Her stomach dropped. Hurriedly wrapping the treasure, she returned it to the cupboard and closed the door.

Dash barked once more then sloped back into the kitchen and flopped onto his rug. He looked at Ruth and whined.

Ruth stood by the range, her arms folded round her middle, quietly listening to the creaks and ticks of the unfamiliar house, trying not to think how far the house was from the main road.

A few minutes later the scullery door slammed shut. Joe burst into the kitchen, his cheeks blotchy with cold. "I saw Uncle Gordon's van going down the track. Did he come to the door?"

Ruth let out a long breath of relief that Joe had returned. "No, he didn't." She glanced at the window.

Joe looked at her for a long moment, then disappeared into the hallway. Ruth followed him, watching as he unlocked the front door and opened it. On the step sat a dish covered with a tea towel, steam curling from its sides.

Joe picked it up, lifted a corner of the tea towel and sniffed. "My uncle's brought us an apple crumble," he said with a small smile.

"But why didn't he knock?" asked Ruth, closing the front door and turning the key. She tugged on the handle to make sure it was locked.

Joe shrugged. "Maybe he wanted to leave the crumble without a fuss, after mum gave him such an earful yesterday. He won't know she's in hospital."

Ruth supposed that did make sense. "You like your uncle, don't you?" she said, the smell of stewed apple making her stomach rumble.

Joe nodded. "I like being around him. He reminds me of my dad," he said quietly.

Ruth thought again of her own dad and his giant bear hugs that made her giggle, his breath smelling of the pear drops he bought with his ration coupons. She let the thought slide away, until the ache in her chest receded.

Later that night Ruth awoke in the dark, a sound pulling her from a deep sleep. A volley of dog barks swept under her bedroom door. She sat up, feeling a curl of unease. Dash's barks were gruff and insistent, just as they had been when Gordon had come to the door earlier that evening. Had he returned? She swung her legs out of bed and listened quietly. Another noise, then the unmistakable crack of breaking glass below her bedroom window.

Quickly climbing from her bed, Ruth crept to the door and placed an ear against it. There was a thud below her bedroom. Dash's howls echoed up the stairs. The skin on the back of her neck crawled. *Someone was downstairs.*

Summoning up all her bravery, Ruth opened her bedroom door and peered down the dark landing. She was relieved to see Joe standing outside his room rubbing his eyes. Audrey's door was closed, and her bedroom light was off. She had returned just after Ruth and Joe had turned in for the night at nine o'clock. Ruth scurried along the carpet to Joe, fear making her body feel as heavy as lead. "I heard glass breaking," she whispered, shivering with cold and fear.

She saw then that Joe was gripping a cricket bat in his right hand. "I heard it too. I'm going downstairs. Stay here," he whispered.

"No. I'll come too," said Ruth, her teeth clattering in her jaw. No matter how scared she was, she couldn't leave him to deal with this alone.

Joe looked at her for a second or two and gave her a quick nod.

Ruth glanced back at Audrey's room. Was she sleeping through this commotion?

They crept down the stairs as quietly as panthers, Ruth's socked feet feeling for each step slowly and cautiously, anxious to avoid any creaks that might alert anyone in the house to their presence.

With a start, she saw a slim figure standing as still as

a statue in the gloom at the foot of the stairs. Her heart cantered in her chest and a strangled scream flew from her lips as Joe raised the cricket bat over his head.

CHAPTER 22

Gone

The figure at the foot of the stairs turned and looked up at them and Ruth gasped in alarm.

"Audrey," hissed Joe, lowering the cricket bat and creeping down the final few steps to stand beside her.

Ruth saw Audrey's face was glowing like a ghostly full moon. "Someone was in the house. But...I think they've gone now," she whispered.

Dash trotted through from the kitchen. He fussed around Audrey's legs. "I woke up and heard Dash barking. I heard glass breaking, footsteps..." she said, her words cracked and small.

"We'll go into the kitchen. On the count of three, I'll switch on the lights," whispered Joe, clutching the bat tighter.

Audrey's bottom lip wobbled. "No, Joe. It could be dangerous. Please put the bat down."

Ruth opened her mouth to protest too, her instincts screaming that if someone was in the house the last thing to do was confront them. But Joe was already lurking in the shadows by the kitchen door. Dash padded into the kitchen again, but this time he didn't bark. Perhaps this was a sign the intruder had been scared off.

Ruth crept over to stand beside Joe.

Audrey was immobile, frozen at the foot of the stairs, pulling in shallow, raspy breaths.

"One, two, three," Joe said under his breath. He burst into the kitchen and flicked on the light switch. The lights flickered and Ruth was afraid they would go out. They flickered once more, then steadied.

Dash stood at the scullery door. He let out three gruff barks. He was agitated now, his eyes bright and alert.

Ruth blinked. There was no one there. Everything was just as they had left it before they'd gone up to bed, except...a bitter breeze swirled round her ankles.

Joe ran past Dash and into the scullery. "The back door's open," he cried in alarm.

Ruth followed him, seeing that one glass pane in the door had been smashed and the key turned from the inside. The house had been broken into.

Joe dropped the bat, pulled on his boots and bolted through the door. Dash howled into the fog. A fresh terror grabbed Ruth by the neck. Whoever had broken in could still be near the house. "Joe, come back!" she called.

Audrey stood next to Ruth, her body visibly trembling. "Please come inside," she cried.

The fog roiled and buffeted, and Ruth grabbed a torch, the beam barely penetrating the thick swathes of white, as if it too had lost its courage. Dash pushed against her legs. She felt the sharpness of the glass under her feet, smelled the cloying damp of the fields drifting inside.

"The glass, Ruth. Please be careful!" exclaimed Audrey, reaching for a broom.

Ruth needed to do something. She needed to get help, but the farm was miles from anywhere and had no telephone. Dash leaned into her side, quivering and panting. It was hopeless.

Audrey swept the glass into a pile in short, sharp strokes and Ruth took a step outside, her socks soon clammy on the wet paving. She shone her torch all around, thinking of the water-filled ditches and Joe running out there alone. Her insides clenched. The torch beam shone on something small, dark and circular at the edge of the paving. She glanced at it, then looked up, distracted by footsteps echoing off the outside walls of the house. The torch beam wavered as her hand shook. Was it Joe, or the intruder? The footsteps were growing closer, and she was too afraid to call out, too afraid to move as Dash barked and barked into the night.

A small figure hurtled from the fog and Ruth felt her shoulders sag with relief. It was Joe. "Come inside, quickly. Did you see anyone?" she asked.

Joe shook his head, his eyes wild. "The fog's so thick, I would never have found them."

"Why would anyone do this?" said Ruth, as they pushed the scullery door closed. The mist swirled around the hole in the jagged glass like smoke.

"I don't know," said Joe grimly. His eyes suddenly widened. He blinked. "Ruth...the treasure."

The sound of Audrey sweeping the broken glass stilled.

Ruth looked at Joe with a slow-dawning horror. But it had to be safe. Nobody knew it was hidden in the dresser cupboard except them.

Ruth ran past Audrey and into the kitchen. She came to a sudden halt. The right-hand door of the dresser cupboard was open. Swallowing a wave of sickness, Ruth rushed over to it and dropped to her knees.

She heard Joe behind her. "No," he whispered.

Ruth reached into the cupboard with shaking hands. *It was empty.* "The pepper pot and ladles are gone," she cried in disbelief.

CHAPTER 23

My Fault

Quiet prickles of fury made Ruth's skin smart as she felt inside the dresser cupboard again, unable to accept that the treasure had been stolen. How had the thief known where to find it? "We must get to a telephone box and call the police," she said thickly.

Joe crouched beside her. "No. I don't want the police here," he said, turning to glance at Audrey.

Audrey's teeth were chattering as she watched, her fingers still curled round the broom handle.

"But the police must be told. The treasure has been stolen," cried Ruth, not understanding.

Audrey's cheeks were ash white. "If the police are called, they may search the farm. That can't happen," she said quietly.

"Why not?" asked Ruth.

Joe stood up. "Terry's keeping petrol in the barn. It's bought on the black market. Mum knows about it, but if the police find out, Terry will get in big trouble."

"Oh," said Ruth, remembering the containers she had seen Terry hide. Even though the war was over, petrol was still rationed because it was in short supply. She remembered one of her friends coming to school and crying because her dad had been caught by the police after storing illegally bought petrol in their garden shed. He had been threatened with prison and a hefty fine, even though the only reason he had bought the petrol was to keep his delivery business going.

Audrey placed a hand to her forehead. "I'm sorry you're involved in this, Ruth. Terry is a good man. It's just…his business is struggling and he needs the petrol for his van. I don't want him to get in trouble."

Ruth nodded. The police could ask awkward questions. And then there was the fact that the treasure didn't belong to the Sterne family in the first place, and the bank was planning on evicting them from the farm next week. What a mess they were in!

The open cupboard door stared at them like a yawning mouth. If only it could speak and tell them what had happened.

Joe was looking at the cupboard too and chewing on his bottom lip. "Who could have done this?"

Ruth rubbed at the spot between her eyebrows and shook her head.

"I need to fix the broken windowpane in the scullery door," said Joe. "There's a piece of tarpaulin in the barn. I'll fetch it and tape it over."

"No. Wait until morning. We'll stop up the gap with an old cloth for now. I'll cycle to Terry's mum's house as soon as it's light. He'll board it over properly," said Audrey.

Hot tears pricked Ruth's eyes as she thought of having to spend the rest of the night in this creaking old farmhouse shrouded in fog. "I don't think I'll be able to sleep upstairs. What if the thief comes back?"

"It'll be all right, Ruth," said Audrey softly.

Ruth turned and saw Audrey's eyes were heavy with tears too. But there was also a glimmer of determination there. "The thief must have got what they came for. They won't be back. You'll be safe here; I'll make sure of it. Let's sleep downstairs with Dash for the rest of the night. We'll all feel better then," she said.

Ruth gave Audrey a wobbly smile, wishing her mum and dad were there to take control. Her mum had said the treasure would be safe in the dresser, but it wasn't. She would be very concerned to learn it had gone. Who could have taken it and why?

Joe and Ruth woke in the kitchen to the sound of Audrey cycling off into the lifting fog, the wheels of her bike skidding on the icy puddles, her head low. She was taking the weight of this family on her shoulders and this break-in had only added to her worries.

"Who could have done this?" asked Ruth for what seemed like the hundredth time, as she walked back from the window and sank into the mound of blankets.

Joe tickled Dash's tummy. "I don't understand how it happened," he said miserably.

"I keep puzzling over how the thief knew where the treasure was," said Ruth. She stared at the window, a shiver of cold dancing across her shoulders as she remembered the feeling of being watched the previous evening as she'd sat examining the treasure at the kitchen table. She had been in full view of anyone who might have been lingering by the window…including Joe's Uncle Gordon, who had left the apple crumble on the doorstep. Ruth suddenly realized she could have unwittingly revealed the treasure's hiding place. Her cheeks flamed with heat, and she chewed on her bottom lip.

"You look all peculiar. What's wrong?" asked Joe.

"There is someone else who might know where the treasure was hidden," Ruth said, quickly telling Joe how she might have been spotted.

Joe's hands stilled from rubbing Dash's tummy. "You think my uncle could have broken into our house and stolen the treasure?"

"I don't know about that. But yesterday I overheard your uncle and the eel man talking by the thicket of trees near Marsh Field. Your uncle was asking for the eel man's help with something. The eel man wasn't happy."

Joe frowned. "Why didn't you mention this yesterday?"

Ruth leaned forward and plucked a few of Dash's coarse black hairs from the blanket. "I suppose I didn't realize how important it was at the time." She glanced at Joe. "The eel man has been watching us at the excavation site. He even asked me yesterday if we'd found anything there. Don't you think that's odd?"

"But that doesn't mean my uncle, or the eel man would steal from us. Uncle Gordon's been trying to help me. You can't accuse someone of doing something without any proof," said Joe, raising his voice a little in disapproval.

Ruth rolled Dash's hairs into a small ball of fluff in her palm as she thought about Joe's words. There had been no sign of anyone by the house last night. But she had seen something unusual. Springing to her feet, she ran through to the scullery and pulled on her boots. Unlocking the door, she stepped out into the cold.

"What are you doing?" asked Joe from the threshold, shivering in his pyjamas.

"Looking for something," said Ruth, who was crouching and looking at the ground. Then she spotted it again. The small circular object she had noticed near the paving the night before. It was black and made of rubber. She picked it up. "I saw this last night, when you were out in the fog looking for the thief. I don't know what it is, but could the thief have dropped it?"

Joe leaned over and took it from Ruth. He turned it over in his hand. "This is an eye guard, from a pair of binoculars. You attach it to the eye piece to stop it rubbing your skin. This one's old, though, you can tell by the way the rubber's falling apart."

"Eel man has binoculars," said Ruth, her stomach swooping. "What if the thing your uncle was asking him to do yesterday *was* to steal the treasure?"

Joe looked doubtful. "But you saw my uncle and eel man in the thicket before you were seen through the window last night. And there must be any number of explanations for why this old eye guard is near the house. Many folks round here use binoculars. It could have blown in from somewhere else."

Ruth's shoulders slumped. Joe was right about all those things. Maybe the eye guard had been there for a while, and it was only the break-in that had made her see it as a potential clue. But she still couldn't help feeling Joe's uncle and the eel man were up to something. "The eel man has been watching us though, Joe. Maybe he saw someone loitering around here, someone suspicious. We should find out."

"You mean pay him a visit?" asked Joe.

"That's exactly what I mean," said Ruth. They had to do something to try and find out what had happened to the treasure and this was the only idea she had.

CHAPTER 24

Telegram

"What a terrible to-do," said Terry, arriving in his van with Audrey an hour later. He shook his head grimly. "I've a piece of wood in my van I'll use to board up the scullery door and make it safe until it can be repaired."

Audrey poured Terry a mug of tea. Her hands trembled and it spilled on the table.

Terry gave her a soft look. "You're exhausted, love. Go and have a lie down."

Audrey shook her head stiffly and Ruth fetched a cloth to wipe up the spillage. "I won't be able to sleep.

Anyway, there's work to be done."

"Have you any news of Mum?" asked Joe, as Ruth mopped up the tea.

"I telephoned the hospital as soon as I woke up. She seems a little better," said Terry. "One of the nurses caught her getting out of bed, insisting she needed to come back to the farm."

Joe grimaced. "That sounds like Mum."

"Poor Mary," said Audrey, letting out a long sigh. "The hospital fees must be upsetting her. I wish I'd insisted she stop work and rest."

"Perhaps we shouldn't tell Mary of the break-in until she's recovered a little. There's nothing she can do from her hospital bed," suggested Terry.

Audrey's eyes filled with tears. She pulled a handkerchief from her apron and wiped her eyes. "I'm so angry about what's happened," she said, her voice small and fierce.

"We all are, love," said Terry.

Ruth wrung out the cloth at the sink, thinking that while Mary would be devastated to learn of the loss of the treasure, she would be even more devastated to learn that the remaining ladle her mum was showing Mr Knight in London belonged to Mr Hartest and couldn't be sold to save the farm. And, that they were facing eviction. She thought of the suggestion she had made to Joe of going to Norwich to try and find Mr Hartest and his notebook. That idea had gone up in smoke – it would be rotten to leave Audrey at the farm alone after the break-in.

"This isn't your fault, Audrey," said Joe, who was shrugging on his coat.

"Joe's right," said Terry, taking a gulp of tea. "The main thing is you're all safe and sound." He paused, looking at Joe. "Thank you for not involving the police."

Joe gave Terry a nod. "Ruth knows by the way… about the petrol in the barn."

"Oh," said Terry, his face tightening in alarm.

"Don't worry, you won't tell, will you, Ruth?" said Joe.

"No, of course not," said Ruth. This was Terry's business and no concern of hers, although it was another secret to add to those already uncovered at the farm.

Audrey kneeled beside Dash, her fingers sweeping over his back in long, smooth strokes. She placed her face against his and he licked her nose.

Terry's eyes darkened. "It's rare to have a break-in

round here. For one thing, people don't own anything worth stealing."

"But the person who broke in knew exactly where the treasure was hidden," said Ruth.

"Well, I told no one about it. And Audrey's good at keeping secrets, aren't you, love?" said Terry.

Audrey nodded, her fingers still combing Dash's fur.

"I'll fetch the wood from your van to board the window before I feed the chickens," Joe said to Terry.

"No, leave it," said Terry, his voice suddenly sharp.

Joe looked up in surprise.

"I'll do it," said Terry, his voice milder. "It's just that I need to get Audrey's bicycle out of the back first and I know where everything is."

While Terry boarded the window and Joe went to fetch the ditch-clearing tools, there was the ring of a bicycle bell outside. "Who's that?" asked Ruth, standing at the window.

"The post boy," said Audrey, walking to the front door. "We don't usually get deliveries this early. Must be a telegram."

As Audrey opened the door, Ruth hovered by the

stairs. Audrey took the telegram and turned. "It's for you, Ruth."

Ruth felt a jolt of concern. It could only be from her mum. Taking it from Audrey and tearing open the envelope, she quickly read it.

Mr Knight keen to see the treasure. He'll drive us to farm early Sat and return us to London after. Hope all well. Mum.

Her mum was bringing Mr Knight to the farm to look at the treasure – but it was gone. Ruth's cheeks flamed with heat.

"Is everything all right?" asked Audrey, her voice etched with concern.

Ruth nodded, folding the telegram and pushing it into her trouser pocket. Except things weren't all right at all. Her jaw clenched with frustration at the mounting problems that needed solving and she strode back into the kitchen to put on her outdoor clothes and find Joe.

CHAPTER 25

The Hut

Ruth and Joe skirted around the back of the house, each carrying a long slubber tool for ditch clearing. A thin pencil line of light separated the fields from the sky as they walked. "This has got to be the right thing to do – we must find out what the eel man knows," said Ruth, feeling for the small rubber binocular eye guard in her coat pocket.

"You really think he'll know something?" asked Joe doubtfully.

Ruth felt fresh resolve as she thought again of the battered binoculars the eel man wore round his neck, the way he had watched the excavation site and asked if anything had been found. "I don't know, but it's Thursday today and with my mum and Mr Knight arriving on Saturday we have to do something, Joe. Imagine driving all that way from London, using all that petrol and finding there is nothing to see."

Joe shook his head grimly. "That wouldn't be good."

They passed on through Rook Field and the trenches Ruth's mum had dug. As they approached the ditch at the far edge of the field, Ruth saw the water tinkled and ran freely, the level significantly lower than it had been when she'd first seen the eel man standing there the day before.

"That's odd," said Joe, staring at the water. "The reeds have been cleared, but Terry was working in Gull Field yesterday."

Ruth shrugged. "Maybe it was Audrey. She was working in the fields too."

Joe nodded. "I suppose. Let's leave the slubber tools on the bridge – there's no point carrying them all the way to the eel man's hut."

Laying her slubber on the narrow wooden bridge leading to Magpie Field, Ruth rubbed her aching arms. "Do you think the eel man will be at home?" she asked, watching for the glint of his binoculars in the reeds, or the barrel of his gun. But the wildfowl swam and chattered peacefully and there was no sign of him.

"It's still early. He might be out hunting," said Joe. "What are we going to say to him, Ruth?"

Ruth followed Joe across the wooden bridge and continued towards the hut, the red corrugated roof glowing like hot coals in the dull-as-dishwater day. "We simply ask him if he knows anything about the break-in." Her words sounded sure and confident, but as they drew closer to the hut Ruth started to feel a little afraid. She glanced back at the farm. It was too far away to see now. How would the eel man react to their arrival and probing questions?

A whisper-thin spiral of smoke wound from the hut's chimney into the air. They picked up their pace, winding through the planted beets, the hut looming closer with every step. Ruth's teeth ached with cold as a hare darted across the field ahead of them, its black-tipped ears flat against its head.

The hut stood on low stilts, perhaps a precaution against the ditches, should they flood.

"Come on then," said Joe, puffing out a breath as they stood looking at the rickety door.

Running lightly up the steps, Ruth knocked twice. There was no reply. Joe knocked again.

"What do we do?" asked Ruth, glancing behind at the bleak landscape. There was no sign of the eel man. She watched as Joe bit on his lower lip and reached for the door handle. It twisted and the door squeaked open. They were met with a rush of fuggy air. "You think we should go inside?" she whispered.

Joe nodded. "Hello, mister. Are you home?" he called, stepping inside the hut. His tentative voice bounced off the wooden walls.

Ruth peered round the door. A small table and single chair sat under the window to the left. On the table lay an assortment of tools, including a hammer. Her breaths quickened. Could the eel man have used it to break the glass in the scullery door before turning the key, coming inside and stealing the treasure?

An ancient black stove ticked quietly in the corner, throwing heat into the hut. It smelled earthy and green inside, of growing things. A long and raggedy maroon curtain hung from the ceiling dividing the hut in two. What was hiding behind there? While Joe silently examined the tools on the table, Ruth walked quickly to the curtain. Her fingers curled round the thick fabric and she slowly drew it back. "Joe...you need to come and see this," she said, her eyes widening at the items spilling out of the crates before her.

CHAPTER 26

Birds

Letting the curtain fall from her fingers, Ruth strode past the woven willow pots stacked one on top of the other, to the crates at the foot of the neatly made single bed. They contained something even more curious than the willow pots – an assortment of woven straw birds.

A peacock peered at them with an imperious glint in its black button eyes. Two woven owls clung to a brown twig, their beaks shaped of stone, their eyes made of tiny orange buttons. A smaller bird, one she could not identify, had been woven so that its head turned to the right at a jaunty angle, as if about to break into a dazzling song. They brought to Ruth's mind the Christmas markets her mum had taken her to visit during the war, where stallholders sold handmade items, keen to make some extra money. "Audrey has a straw bird like this. What are they for?" Ruth asked Joe in amazement.

"The eel man makes and sells them at local markets," said Joe.

A loud crack outside startled them both. It was followed by the squawks and caws of scattering birds. Ruth ran to the window and peered out. Wildfowl careened into the grey sky. Joe stood beside her, his fingers gripping the edge of the table.

The eel man stood on the bridge holding his gun. He stared at the ground. He must be looking at their slubbers. Ruth saw him look up and glance towards the hut. He hoisted his gun over one shoulder, a bulging sack over the other and began to march towards them.

"He's coming, Joe," said Ruth, feeling a shudder of fear. They had not come here with the best of intentions.

Joe opened the hut door. The eel man stopped and stared at them both. His eyes darkened and Ruth thought she saw his grip tighten round the gun.

Keeping his eyes on them, he quickly strode on.

Ruth's heart hammered uncomfortably as she watched him draw near. Joe said nothing, but his breathing had quickened, puffing like smoke into the razor-thin air.

The eel man dropped the sack at the foot of the steps and leaned his gun against the outside wall. Walking up the steps, he brushed past Ruth and Joe as he came inside without saying a word. Closing the door behind them all, he glanced at the pulled-back curtain, then walked to the stove. Easing off his fingerless gloves, he rested a palm on the side of a black kettle. "Water's still warm. Tea?"

Ruth felt a jolt of surprise.

Joe blinked.

Ruth's eyes flicked to the hammer on the table. She needed to find out if the eel man knew anything about the stolen treasure. But now she was here she was struggling to find the right words.

The eel man followed Ruth's gaze to the hammer and his slug-like eyebrows tugged together. He poured hot water into a cracked brown teapot, stirred it, then made the tea in three dented tin mugs. Placing them on the table, he gestured for Ruth and Joe to each take one.

Ruth approached the table cautiously. The tea was stewed, thick and black. She took a sip and let the heat loosen the knot in her throat.

"You think it's me who broke in to your house?" the eel man asked Joe gruffly, nodding at the hammer.

"But…how do you know about the break-in?" asked Joe, giving Ruth an uncertain glance.

"I have eyes and ears in my head, lad. And a pair of these." Eel Man pointed to the binoculars hanging round his neck. As Ruth stared at them, she saw that one of the binocular eye guards was missing. Joe was staring at the binoculars too and a slow flush was stealing over his cheeks.

"Something's been found in the field – something valuable judging by what I've seen. Is that what someone was after?" said the eel man.

"You've been watching the farm," said Ruth, feeling a growing anger. She placed her mug on the table. "Why would you do that? Was it you who took the treasure? Did Joe's uncle ask you to steal it?" She pulled the binocular eye guard from her pocket and laid it in her palm. "I found this near the house," she said, her fingers shaking a little.

Joe threw Ruth another worried look.

The surprise in eel man's face tightened the crevices in his cheeks. "Gordon asked me to help Joe's family. Not steal from them." He looked at the eye guard in Ruth's palm. "My eye guards are old; this one must have fallen off one of the times I walked by to check if everything was all right, just as Gordon asked."

Ruth clenched the eye guard into her fist. "Gordon asked you to help?" she said hesitantly.

"But…I don't understand," said Joe.

The crevices in the eel man's face deepened. "Your uncle was afraid to offer help as Mary won't accept anything from him. Gordon's been paying me for a while to do what I can on the farm, clear ditches and the like. But he said Mary mustn't know. I was worried about it – thought it better she knew what was happening."

Ruth rearranged in her head the conversation she had overheard between the eel man and Gordon in the thicket the day before. She had thought Gordon was asking the eel man to do something bad. But maybe Gordon did want to help the family, just like Joe had said. Nothing was quite as it seemed on the farm, and she was learning that appearances could be very deceptive.

"The ditch bordering Magpie and Rook Fields, did you clear the reeds from it?" Joe asked.

The eel man nodded. "Bulrushes and silt were choking it, stopping the water flow. I'm doing what I can, in between hunting. Just enough to help, but not enough to make your mum suspect someone's been interfering."

Ruth hung her head and felt very ashamed. "I'm sorry we came into your hut uninvited. It's just...I thought..." Her voice faltered. The eel man sidled over to the crate of straw birds and selected a swan. He held it out to Ruth. "Go on, missy. Take it."

Ruth looked at him.

"Go on," he urged again, giving her a small smile. "I want you to have it."

Ruth took a tentative step forward and took the swan from him quickly.

"Making these birds keeps me busy on long winter nights," the eel man said, his voice a little lighter than before.

Ruth stroked a finger over the delicate straw braiding. It seemed incongruous that someone who lived such a harsh life on the land could also make something so beautiful.

"I don't like suffering, but hunting is how I survive. Might seem daft to you, but when I weave the straw, it feels like I'm binding together little pieces of the birds' souls," he said, his cheeks reddening. "I find weaving soothing; it takes me far away from my worries."

Ruth had heard her dad say that painting helped take him away from his worries too. She was surprised to find a similarity between the eel man and her own family. She was hit with a sudden understanding. The skin by the eel man's eyes was wrinkled, his cheeks leathery and as thread-veined as a spider's web. He lived a hard life on the land, but he was also connected to it. She didn't know how things worked in this part of the country, and rather than listening and learning she had jumped to conclusions, thinking he might have been involved with the break-in. "Thank you for the swan," she said, really meaning it. "Audrey has one just like it. I'm Ruth by the way."

"I'm Lenny," he replied, giving her a nod.

"Lenny," said Joe with a slow smile. "Dad never told me your name."

"I'm the eel man to everyone nowadays, but I sometimes like to hear the sound of the name my ma gave me," said Lenny, his eyes twinkling. The twinkle dulled a little. "I gave Audrey the swan to try and cheer her up. I see her crying by the ditches sometimes. It saddens me."

"Oh," said Ruth. Audrey kept any sadness she was feeling well hidden.

"I've told Gordon about the break-in. We're going to keep an eye on the farm and ask around, see what we can find out," said Lenny. He shook his head. "Your family are down on their luck, Joe. Have been for some time."

"Mum's in hospital," said Joe, dipping his head.

Lenny rubbed his chin. "Explains why I didn't see her out in the fields yesterday. I'm sorry, lad. I really am."

Lenny really did seem to care about the Sterne family. Perhaps there was something else he might know that could help them out of the muddle they were in. "Do you know a Mr Hartest who sometimes visited Joe's dad?" asked Ruth, stroking the straw bird's feather-light tail.

Lenny took a slurp of tea. "I do. Haven't seen him in these parts for some years now."

"The person who broke in to the house took some things my dad was keeping safe for Mr Hartest," said Joe glumly.

Lenny placed his mug on the table. "I think you'd better explain from the beginning." He folded his arms and listened carefully as Ruth and Joe told him how Mr Hartest had not returned for his treasure, even though he had promised in his letter to come back and excavate the site where Joe's dad had found the spearhead and glass beads. Ruth told Lenny about her mum and Mr Knight arriving on Saturday to see the treasure, which had now been stolen. She also explained how she thought finding Mr Hartest's notebook might be the answer to their problems.

Joe took a deep breath. "There's something else. But you need to promise not to tell my uncle or Audrey, as Mum needs to hear it from me first."

Lenny nodded solemnly and Joe told him about the eviction letters from the bank and the threat of losing Rook Farm the very next week.

Lenny shook his head grimly. "Things are worse than your uncle or I could have ever imagined. It seems to me Ruth is right. You have Mr Hartest's last-known address so you must see if you can find him and his notebook." He turned to Ruth. "I imagine your mother and the museum man would be keen to see this notebook too."

Ruth grimaced. "But we can't leave Audrey alone, not after everything that's happened."

Lenny gave a brisk nod. "Let me speak to Gordon. I'm sure he'll send some workers to help harvest the beet when he hears Mary is so unwell. And you needn't worry. I'll keep everything you've said to myself. I agree Mary needs to hear this from your lips, Joe."

Ruth pushed the straw swan into her coat pocket and felt a rising hope. Joe's face had brightened too. The theft of Mr Hartest's treasure had brought things to a head – but at least the secrets were being shared now.

CHAPTER 27

Bus

Ruth and Joe flagged down the Norwich bus early the next morning, just as the sun began to peep through the soup-like mist.

The driver's moustache twitched as they climbed aboard. "Aren't you the early birds? Off on a day trip?"

"Something like that," said Joe, as Ruth paid for two return tickets and waited for her change.

As they settled into their seats, Ruth thought about Joe's uncle Gordon, who had arrived at Rook Farm that morning with his workers to help with the beet harvest. Joe had greeted them in the yard, and Gordon had put a kindly arm round Joe's shoulders as they talked. Ruth felt glad, hoping this was a first step towards them working together to help save the farm. But there was still the problem of the looming eviction, which Joe was keeping a secret. She had suggested he tell his uncle, but Joe had refused, saying again that his mum must hear about it from him.

Ruth rested her head on the seat back as the bus bumped along the rutted road, realizing they were both fast running out of time. It was Friday, which meant the bank would arrive to claim the farm early the next week, if the loan could not be repaid. And tomorrow her mum and Mr Knight were arriving, expecting to see the pepper pot and ladles. Mr Knight's disappointment at learning they had been stolen would be huge and Ruth's stomach rolled over whenever she imagined how her mum's face would fall when she told her. The challenges were great if she thought about them too hard. They were pinning their hopes on a man who hadn't been seen for six years, and his notebook leading them to where the beads and spearhead had been found and potentially more treasure. Quite frankly it was barmy. She gritted her teeth and tried to push the negative thoughts away. She needed to concentrate on the day ahead and doing all she could to help Joe's family and her own.

"I wonder if Audrey has read the note we left yet?" asked Joe, cutting through Ruth's thoughts.

"I hope she's not too upset," said Ruth with a grimace. She hadn't been happy about leaving a vague note on the kitchen table saying they would be gone for the day and not to worry, but both she and Joe had agreed it was better to keep the purpose of their day out to themselves, rather than raise hopes. It would only cause more disappointment if they failed in their task.

The first stop on the way to Norwich was Ely and Ruth drew in a breath at the sight of the cathedral rising through the fog in the distance, like a magnificent ship. "Look at that," she said, wiping the condensation on the window with her coat sleeve.

"Sometimes Dad used to drive me to Ely on a Saturday. We'd visit the sweet shop," said Joe ruefully.

"You must miss that," Ruth said quietly.

Joe nodded and continued to gaze out of the window. The bus wheels bounced and their shoulders bumped together. "Since Dad died, Mum's made all the decisions at the farm. What I think doesn't seem to matter. That was another reason why I didn't want to tell Mum about the eviction letters and Mr Hartest's treasure. I wanted to sort those things on my own. But I failed."

"You haven't failed. You've had some jolly big problems that are far too big for you to sort out on your own," said Ruth. She grinned and nudged him. "It's a good job I'm here to help."

Joe smiled too. "Except you thought my uncle and Lenny had stolen the treasure and found a clue that wasn't a clue at all."

Ruth laughed. "Are you saying I'm not a good detective?"

Joe laughed along with her. "I reckon I am saying that, yes." His face became more serious. "I'm glad you're here, Ruth."

"I'm glad I'm here too," said Ruth, feeling a warm glow of friendship, for that was what Joe was quickly becoming – a friend. She gave him a sidelong glance. "Do you have many friends at school?"

Joe wrinkled his nose. "My friend Fred passed his eleven-plus examination and he's at the grammar school now. I failed mine, so I'm at the secondary modern. Fred visited the farm a few times after my dad died, but it felt strange. I didn't know what to say. He didn't either."

Ruth gave him a sympathetic look. "Some of my friends didn't know what to say when they found out my mum and dad were getting divorced. Mum said the most important thing was to be honest about how I was feeling."

Joe picked at a few flecks of mud on his gloves. "Change is hard, isn't it? There's been so much of it since the war ended. I know the farm must change if it's to make more money. I'm determined to make my mum see that now."

"Change doesn't have to be a bad thing," said Ruth, thinking of London. While progress was slow in some areas, like the clearing of bomb damage and rebuilding of homes, in other areas things were changing at a rapid pace. "A new shop opened in London this year. It's self-service, so you can help yourself to the different things on the shelves and pay for them all together before you leave. It sells all sorts of food, so you don't have to go to the baker, grocer and butcher. Mum thinks it's a good thing and will speed up shopping trips, but Dad says it will never catch on. The point is though that things are going to keep on changing whether we like it or not," said Ruth.

Joe flashed Ruth a warm smile. "I'm going to ask

Uncle Gordon to show me how to use the tractor in the barn and prove to Mum it will be a good for the farm. You're helping me to accept things need to be different. I just hope Mum gets better quickly and can come home soon."

A small boy in the seat in front was offered a sweet by his dad. Father and son pressed their heads together, the brown paper bag rustling as the boy rummaged inside. Ruth swallowed. While she was good at giving advice, she was not so good at taking it. "I'm not sure I'll ever get used to my life changing and my dad not living with us."

"After my dad died, some days my stomach felt so twisted I could barely breathe. But you've still got your dad, Ruth," said Joe. He said it as a matter of fact and not at all unkindly. "It doesn't hurt so much to think about Dad now. The farm was part of him and I like knowing I'll carry on what he started."

Ruth thought about Joe's words as she looked out of the bus window towards the approaching town. He was right. Her dad had survived the war and she could still see him whenever she liked. She was very grateful for that. She also admired Joe's commitment to the farm. Ruth had never thought beyond her life in London, sometimes feeling it was a place she would never leave. Her mum had chosen to pursue a job she loved, and so had Joe and she saw how important this was. It made her think of her own future. Perhaps she could also work outside, where she could breathe in crisp air and feel her muscles ache after a day of hard work. She didn't know what this future life looked like yet, but perhaps just knowing there was the possibility of doing something different, somewhere different, was enough.

The bus swerved, jostling Ruth towards the aisle. The other passengers muttered and tutted. Ruth and Joe peered over the seat backs to the driver, who was shaking his head. He brought the bus to a slow stop beside a row of terraced cottages.

"What's happened?" asked Ruth, feeling worried.

"Flat tyre, I reckon," said Joe.

The bus driver went to inspect the outside of the bus and it was just as Joe had suspected. "Sorry, folks," the driver said a short while later after climbing aboard again. "I'll need to call the garage and get the tyre repaired. You'll have to get off here and wait for the next bus. It could be a few hours."

Groans and mutters filled the air as people picked

up bags, put on hats and shuffled down the aisle and out into the cold.

"A few hours! We can't wait that long," exclaimed Ruth. They had to make sure they caught the last bus back from Norwich and this would not allow them enough time.

"Trains run between Ely and Norwich. But could we afford the fare?" asked Joe.

Ruth quickly counted the remaining coins in her coat pocket. "We might just have enough to get us there and buy a cup of tea."

"Then that's what we'll do. Come on, we're not giving up now," said Joe, his eyes fiery. "We've got to see if we can find Mr Hartest and his notebook before your mum arrives at the farm tomorrow with Mr Knight."

Ruth grinned. Joe seemed to have the bit between his teeth now and it was good to see.

CHAPTER 28

Belvoir Street

After a brisk walk to Ely station, Ruth bought their tickets and learned they had a forty-five-minute wait for the Norwich-bound train. She shivered and stamped her feet on the platform to warm her toes.

"There's a tearoom round the back of the station where we could wait," said Joe, rubbing his arms.

"Good idea," said Ruth. It would mean spending the last of their money, but if she didn't warm up soon her limbs would turn into icicles, and they might not make it to Norwich at all.

The windows of Hilda's tearoom were steamy with

condensation. Inside, they were greeted with the smell of coffee and the sweetness of freshly baked buns. The woman behind the counter was icing the buns with a piping bag, her tongue sticking out to one side in concentration. "Can I help?" she said eventually, looking up.

"Two mugs of tea, please," said Ruth, her stomach groaning at the sight of the buns.

The woman saw her eyeing them. "And two of these? Fresh this morning."

Ruth felt the few leftover coins in her pocket. "Um. They look delicious, but no thank you."

The woman smiled. "Take a seat and I'll bring the tea over. You look like you need it. This chill has set in from the east and it's supposed to snow tomorrow." She gave Joe a long look, then turned back to the tea urn.

Joe chose them a couple of seats close to a small fire glowing gently in the grate. Ruth pulled off her hat and gloves and warmed her fingers.

"Here you are," said the woman, carrying over a tray. Next to the teas were two iced buns topped with glistening glacé cherries. "Oh, I can't afford to pay for those…" Ruth began.

The woman smiled and placed them on the table anyway. "I don't expect you to. I know who you are," she said, nodding at Joe. "You're Mary and Roy's boy."

Joe looked surprised.

"I'm Hilda. I went to school with your mum," she said. "I moved to London but came back during the war. I see your mum's Land Girl in here every month. Audrey's always welcome."

Hilda pulled something from her apron pocket. "In fact, could you please return this to her? I know she'll be back in a few weeks, but it's been bothering me that she dropped it. It fell out of the book she was reading."

"Of course," said Joe with a smile, taking it from Hilda.

Ruth saw it was a photograph.

"And you tell Audrey not to worry about spending her whole day off sitting here reading. She always pays her way and it's no bother to me. I like the company," said Hilda.

Joe stared at Hilda. "She spends her whole day off here?"

"Why yes. Every four weeks as regular as clockwork. She says she likes being somewhere quiet, where she can think. I keep the place warm too with the extra coal my brother finds me," she whispered, gesturing at the fire and giving them a wink.

The doorbell jangled and a new customer entered the tearoom. Hilda flashed Ruth and Joe a smile and hurried back to the counter.

Joe placed the photograph on the table, gave it a lingering look then picked up his bun and took a big bite.

Ruth slid the black-and-white photograph towards her. A family stood in front of a large, detached villa on an expanse of lawn. A woman was lounging in a striped deckchair grinning broadly. Two girls, perhaps in their late teens, dressed in shorts and blouses, were doing handstands next to her, while two cows poked their heads over a low hedge behind them. Turning it over, she saw some faint writing on the back. *Audrey, Emma and Mum. Villa Gardens, Martineau Lane, Norwich.* Looking at the photograph again, she felt certain one of the girls was Audrey. The other must be her sister Emma. Audrey had said her home was in the city, so perhaps this had been taken at a friend's or relative's house.

"What Hilda said just now was odd. Audrey says she goes to visit her family in Norwich once a month. But instead, she sits here all day," said Joe through a mouthful of bun.

Ruth placed the photograph on the table and took a sip of tea. "You think Audrey doesn't visit her family?"

Joe shrugged.

"How peculiar. Could they have had a falling-out? Lenny did say he sometimes sees Audrey crying alone in the fields," said Ruth.

"I'm not sure. She hasn't mentioned anything like that," said Joe, taking the cherry from his cake and nibbling it, keen to make it last as long as possible.

Ruth took a bite of her own bun, the sugary sweetness aching her gums. She thought of Audrey's sister Emma and the name charms Audrey didn't wear on her bracelet. It was all rather puzzling.

The Norwich-bound train was on time and the journey blissful in the heated carriage. "Look," said Joe, peering out of the window as they approached the outskirts of the city. The train juddered and rocked past a row of terraced housing interspersed by vacant land piled high with rubble. Signs of the war still scarred the landscape here, just like in London.

"Bomb sites," said Ruth dully.

Joe pressed his nose to the glass. "I've only seen photographs of them in newspapers, and on the newsreel when my brother Billy took me to the pictures once or twice."

Ruth grimaced. "We arrived at school one morning and the whole of one wall was missing. You could see straight into my classroom and the blackboard with equations from our math's lesson the day before."

Joe's eyes widened. "My dad sometimes felt guilty he hadn't gone to fight and that we didn't face the same troubles as people living in towns and cities. But he worked all hours to increase the crops we grew to help feed the country. It must have been frightening living in London."

"I think you get used to anything after a time," said Ruth. "I don't remember the war beginning and it was odd when the air-raid sirens stopped."

"The Luftwaffe sometimes flew over our farm on a bombing run," said Joe darkly. "You'd hear the low drone of the German bombers approaching, a bit like hornets. Dad would run out into the yard. He kept a pile of beets by the front door and he'd hurl them at the sky. 'Take that!' he'd cry, as the beets splatted on the concrete. Dash would dance round his legs, thinking it was a game."

Ruth smiled. It felt good to share stories of the war. It also made her realize how very different their experiences had been.

After asking a man at the train-station ticket office for directions to Belvoir Street – Mr Hartest's address – the children set off. The half-hour walk led them through Chapelfield Gardens, where a few families braved the cold, and onwards past a Catholic cathedral which loomed in the gunmetal grey sky. It was strange to be surrounded by the hubbub of a city again after the remoteness of the farm, and Ruth found she missed the quietness and wind whistling across the acres of flat fields. The farm was isolated, but she saw that also made it special.

A truck rumbled past and Joe glanced up at it and gasped. "There's a house on the back of that vehicle."

Ruth stared too. It was a new single-storey prefabricated house, like the ones she had seen going up in London. They were a quick and temporary solution to house the many people who had been made homeless in the war.

"It's fully built. Look, you can see there's a green bath and toilet. There's even a kitchen with a sink and taps!" said Joe with a sudden laugh.

It made Ruth smile too, but it also caused a thought to pop into her head. "If they are putting those prefabs up round here, that means this area must have been badly bombed."

"The war's been over for almost three years. How can it take so long to make these repairs?" said Joe, peering down the street.

"Mum thinks I'll be grown up before all the rubble is cleared and new buildings are put up," said Ruth. Very little had been done to repair and rebuild the places that had been bombed in their part of London. Rebuilding a destroyed world took time, money, and people, and the last two of those things were in very short supply.

They headed off down Belvoir Street, passing the row of terraces in silence, glancing at the door numbers as they walked. The truck carrying the ready-made house had rumbled on, past a grocer's shop and across another street where the shouts of workmen operating a crane could be heard.

As they approached the grocer's, Ruth was filled with a dark dismay. The house numbers zigzagged up the street, odd numbers on one side, even on the other. Number seventy-three was on the opposite side of the road, where Belvoir Street continued. Except the street didn't continue. The buildings were gone on both sides of that part of the street – they'd been bombed out in the war. Prefabricated houses were being erected on the vacant site.

Joe's shoulders slumped.

"This explains why you couldn't reach Mr Hartest on the telephone, and why your letters weren't answered," said Ruth feeling cold. "His part of Belvoir Street was destroyed in the war."

"All the houses are gone. Mr Hartest's house and his neighbours' houses too," said Joe, his voice tight.

Ruth and Joe crossed over the street and watched the crane creak and clank as it prepared to lift the prefab house onto its concrete standing. A small group of people had gathered to watch. "Perhaps someone over there might know what happened to him?" Ruth said, pointing out the onlookers.

Walking towards the huddle of people, Ruth singled out a kind-faced woman in a brown sheepskin coat. A small girl stood by her side sucking on a liquorice stick. "Excuse me," Ruth said shyly.

"Yes?" said the woman, bending down to wipe the girl's sticky lips.

"We're looking for someone who used to live here. Mr Hartest. He lived at number seventy-three."

The woman's face fell as she gestured to the vacant site. "Houses on this part of the street were destroyed in the Baedeker raids six years ago this April. I know some people lost their lives, but it was before I moved to the area."

Ruth swallowed. Her mum had told her the Germans had targeted historic cities in Britain listed in a Baedeker guidebook, which gave the name to these particularly vicious raids. Historic buildings and archaeological sites had been deliberately bombed in an attempt to weaken people's spirits. The Luftwaffe had also bombed Bath during these raids, where some of the British Museum's relics were stored for safekeeping in a quarry. Ruth's mum had been very afraid that the precious artefacts would be destroyed. They had survived. However, many buildings in Bath were damaged, just like in Norwich and the other cities targeted. And of course, many people's lives were lost as well.

"I'm sorry if that news upsets you," said the woman, looking with concern at Joe's white-as-chalk face.

"It's all right. Thank you for your help," said Ruth, pulling on Joe's coat sleeve and moving away. They crossed back over the street and leaned against the wall of the grocer's shop next to a crate of wizened potatoes.

Ruth's dismay deepened as the crane winched the house into position exactly where Mr Hartest's home had once stood. The whole street had gone. Had he and his neighbours all perished in the bombing raid? Being in Norwich was a stark reminder that the war might be over, but the losses had been enormous and things would never be the same again.

CHAPTER 29

Sally

"Poor Mr Hartest. I wonder what happened the night of the raids?" said Ruth glumly. The prefabricated house had been lowered into place and she and Joe watched as the crowd of onlookers began to drift away.

Joe's shoulders were stooped as he leaned against the wall of the grocer's shop.

Ruth's stomach gurgled and she folded her arms round her middle. It was a long while since they'd eaten their buns in Ely and it would also be a long while before they arrived back at the farm for tea. She glanced at the crates of feeble vegetables outside the shop. Perhaps the few remaining coins she had in her pocket would buy them some fruit to lift their mood.

Inside the shop there was no fruit to be found, however. Ruth and Joe stood for a while looking longingly at a tin of golden syrup and an enticing packet of chocolate biscuits on the ration shelf. But they didn't have enough money and, in any case, they'd need a ration book registered with the shop in order to buy anything.

The shopkeeper behind the counter glanced up from organizing packets of soap. "Can I help you?" he asked, pushing his glasses onto his nose.

"Um…no. Thank you anyway," said Ruth heading for the door.

"Actually, you might be able to help," Ruth heard Joe say to the man.

She turned and looked at him. To her surprise she saw Joe had the same look of intent as he'd had in Ely when suggesting they caught the train.

"We're in Norwich for the day to try and find one of my dad's friends. Mr Hartest. He lived on this street, the part that got bombed out," said Joe.

The shopkeeper's eyebrows tugged together in

sympathy. "I took on the shop after the war. I'm afraid I don't know anyone by the name of Hartest. Did your father know him well?"

Joe looked downcast. "They were friends, but my dad's passed on now."

"Oh. I am sorry to hear that," said the shopkeeper, tilting his head to one side.

Thanking the man for his time, Ruth and Joe stepped back out into the cold.

Ruth adjusted her scarf. The air was bitter, the grey clouds hanging low in the sky. "It was worth a try," she said.

Joe shrugged, looking miserable. "I can't think how else we can find out what happened to Mr Hartest. I suppose we'd better head back to the bus station."

They set off down the street in glum silence. Ruth thought about Mr Knight arriving in his car the next day. She shook her head in exasperation at the thought of his bottom lip curling in displeasure at her and her mum, once he discovered he had driven all that way to see nothing but fields of beet and that the treasure hadn't belonged to the farm in the first place.

"Hello...you two over there...could you hang on a moment."

Ruth and Joe turned. The shopkeeper they had just spoken to was marching down the street after them, his blue apron flapping.

"What do you think he wants?" asked Joe.

"I have no idea," said Ruth, stepping aside to give a wide berth to a woman being taken for a walk by a large black dog.

The shopkeeper caught them up, his chest heaving. He took off his glasses and wiped them on his apron. "The man you mentioned in the shop. You said he lived on the bombed-out part of this street?"

Joe nodded.

"Well…it's just that the King family used to live on that part of the street. They come into my shop quite regularly. Mrs King has spoken before of how her home was destroyed in an air raid. Maybe she would know what happened to your father's friend?" said the shopkeeper, putting his glasses on.

Ruth's eyes brightened. "Do you think she would mind talking to us?" she asked.

"Let's find out, shall we? She lives just over there now," the shopkeeper said, pointing to a terraced property with a grey door a little way down the street.

Ruth and Joe exchanged hopeful glances as the

shopkeeper took them to the house and knocked on Mrs King's door. The door opened a few seconds later. It wasn't Mrs King who opened the door though. It was a girl, a bit older than Ruth and Joe, who was wearing a thick coat, purple woolly hat and matching gloves.

"Hello, Sally. Is your mum in?" said the shopkeeper.

"No, she's out," Sally said, giving Ruth and Joe a curious look.

"Oh. I see you're on your way out too. I'm sorry to bother you," said the shopkeeper.

Sally tugged at the fingers of one of her gloves. "I'm not going out. I can't switch on the electric fire until after four o'clock. Have to keep warm somehow."

Ruth threw Sally a sympathetic look. She certainly knew how that felt.

"Can I pass on a message?" Sally asked.

"Yes, please," said the shopkeeper, turning to Joe. "This boy's father knew a man who lived on Belvoir Street. They're trying to find out what happened to him. Mr Harson, was it?"

"Mr Hartest," said Ruth and Joe at the exact same time.

Sally's expression changed from curiosity to shock.

"Your dad knew Mr Hartest?" she said, stepping outside and pulling the door to.

Ruth and Joe exchanged a glance.

Joe nodded. "Did you…know him?"

"We were next-door neighbours," said Sally.

Ruth's eyes widened and Joe shook his head in disbelief.

The shopkeeper smiled. "I'm glad I could be of help, but I must get back to the shop," he said backing away. "Bye then."

"Thank you so much," called Ruth.

"Yes, thank you," echoed Joe, quickly going on to explain to Sally how Mr Hartest had been a regular visitor at Rook Farm and how he'd talked to his dad about old things. "Mr Hartest had this notebook. We were keen to talk to him and find out what happened to it."

Sally frowned. "Sorry. I don't know about any notebook, but I can tell you what happened to Mr Hartest." She glanced back up the street towards the part that had been bombed.

Ruth felt a familiar dismay, becoming fearful for what they were about to learn. "Thank you. I'm Ruth and this is Joe. We're only here for the day and it's very kind of you to help us."

Sally smiled. "I'm happy to help if I can. I was friends with Meg, Mr Hartest's daughter. Sometimes we'd go out with her dad when he went looking."

"Looking?" said Ruth, not understanding.

"Yes, you know. Looking for old things buried in the ground," Sally said. "But he only looked for things on his days off. He worked at Colman's – the mustard factory, just like my mum and dad and a few others on the street. He volunteered at the Castle Museum too." She smiled at the memory. "He must have really loved old things to want to spend so much time with them."

Ruth smiled too as she thought of her mum's passion for the past and Joe's dad and his love of old things.

"Anyway, it was the night of the raid it all went wrong," continued Sally, her eyes darkening. "The sirens began blaring just after midnight. Mum hurried us downstairs. I got a right telling-off for accidentally treading on her daffodils as we made our way to the Anderson shelter in our back garden. We shared the shelter with the Hartest family, you see, as their garden was smaller than ours. It was freezing down there, smelled horribly damp too. All I wanted was to climb back into my warm bed."

Ruth's throat constricted. Sally's words were bringing back vivid memories of nights spent sheltering underground in London from the air raids.

"My mum and dad insisted we stay until the all-clear siren had sounded," Sally continued. "But then Meg realized they'd forgotten their cat, Tiggy. Her dad decided to go back to the house to look for Tiggy. Turns out she was fine, but then the bomb dropped," said Sally looking downcast.

"How dreadful," whispered Ruth.

"The shelter shook, my ears popped and Meg and I began to cry. Even my dad looked frightened," said Sally.

"What a terrible thing," said Joe shaking his head.

"Dreadful," said Ruth, whose brain was grappling with the unwelcome image of Mr Hartest dashing through the dark as bombs whistled to the ground. "Did...did Mr Hartest get out of the house in time?"

Sally sniffed and shook her head slowly. "I'm sorry to say he didn't."

Ruth glanced at Joe, who seemed quite stricken by this awful news. She reached out and touched him lightly on the arm, wanting to comfort him somehow.

Joe pulled in a deep breath and cleared his throat.

"We haven't heard from Mr Hartest for six years. I did wonder whether something had happened to him in the war, but I still had a bit of hope. To find out the full story…well…it's hard to take in."

Sally sighed. "It was a terrible time. But you should know that Meg and her mum did survive the raid."

Joe looked a little brighter. "Do you think Mrs Hartest would be willing to speak with us? I would like to pay my respects," he said, pulling his hat more firmly over his ears.

"The family moved away," said Sally, pulling a loose thread from a glove and holding it up like a worm.

"Oh," said Joe, his face falling.

Sally pushed the wool into her coat pocket. "They didn't go far though. You'll find Meg's mum working at Bond's, that's a shop just off Ber Street. Although the shop was bombed out. It isn't there any more."

"Then why would we find Mrs Hartest working there?" asked Ruth, feeling confused.

"Because Mr Bond didn't let the Luftwaffe get the better of him," said Sally with a sudden laugh, as if it were the most obvious thing in the world. "I'll take you there now if you like."

"Yes, please," said Ruth, taking some solace from the

fact they would at least be able to speak with Mr Hartest's wife. Then she felt a jolt of concern. They were also going to have to tell Mrs Hartest that most of the treasure her husband had hidden from the Germans at Rook Farm was not safe at all and had been stolen. That would be a very difficult conversation indeed.

CHAPTER 30

Mr Bond's Buses

Ruth, Joe and Sally stood looking at the derelict site where Bond's department store had once stood. Reminders of the devastation and destruction of war hung over the street like a dark cloud.

"I heard that a new line of perfume might be arriving today," Ruth heard one woman say to another as they brushed past, scarfs pulled tight round their necks.

"I do admire Mr Bond," said the other woman. "It's optimistic people like him who make me proud of this country and sure that we'll recover."

Sally beckoned Joe and Ruth forward and the three

of them followed the two chattering women. "Come and see what Mr Bond has done. I think it's champion." Taking a left turn, she led them into a concrete car park. As Ruth took in her surroundings, she realized Sally was right. This was indeed champion. Red-and-cream single-decker buses stood in parallel lines, with wooden wedges propped against their wheels to prevent them from moving. Light bulbs had been strung between the buses, giving a merry and almost festive feel.

Stacks of kitchen utensils, pots and pans, buckets and mops stood outside one bus. In the window of another bus, dresses, skirts and jackets hung on rails. Three prams were parked to the side of the bus to their left, where mums, with small mewling children on their hips, examined racks of tiny shoes, knitted cardigans and blankets.

Joe and Ruth looked at each other and smiled. They were surrounded by the hustle and bustle of a market, except this was no ordinary market. Somehow Mr Bond had set up his bombed-out store in a fleet of buses and the effect was rather magical.

"See," said Sally with a smile. "I told you it was champion."

"It sure is," said Joe, whistling through his teeth.

"Do you know which bus Mrs Hartest works on?" asked Ruth.

"Cosmetics," said Sally. "Barbara always did like working around nice things. She can't afford much and says it's the next best thing to owning them herself. Although I can't imagine there's much on sale what with all the shortages."

Ruth followed Sally's pointed finger to a bus at the far end of the car park, next to a corrugated tin shed that was operating as a café. A few customers were warming their hands on hot drinks.

As they walked to the bus, Ruth hung back and gestured for Joe to do the same. "I feel a bit nervous now we're here."

"Me too. But we must do this," said Joe, pushing his shoulders back, taking off his hat and stuffing it into his pocket.

Sally stood on tiptoes to look through the bus window. Ruth saw a woman inside opening her purse to pay for the goods she had bought. Shortly after, she exited the bus, giving them a friendly nod as she left.

"Best go in now before more customers arrive," said Sally, running up the steps of the bus.

Ruth and Joe followed her inside. The seats had been

241

stripped out and replaced with long counters where a few rows of lipsticks stood like shiny soldiers and several bottles of perfume and a rack of jewellery jostled for attention.

A woman wearing a black skirt and blue cardigan looked up and smiled brightly when she saw Sally. "Hello, love. This is a nice surprise." Her eyes drifted to Ruth and Joe and then back to Sally. "You've brought some friends with you?"

"Um, not exactly. Joe, here, knew Colin. He wanted to pay his respects. I hope you don't mind me bringing them over," said Sally.

"Oh," said Mrs Hartest, stepping out from behind the makeshift counter. She was younger than Ruth had imagined she would be, perhaps in her thirties. Her brown hair was fashionably curled but her carefully applied make-up failed to disguise the shadows under her eyes.

"I'll leave you to it if that's all right. I think I'll have a look round some of the buses now I'm here – it's Mum's birthday next month. It was nice to meet you, Ruth, Joe. Goodbye, Barbara," said Sally, giving them a cheery wave.

Ruth and Joe waved goodbye too, thanking Sally

again for her help, and turned back to Mrs Hartest, who was looking at them with interest.

"It's kind of you to stop by, but my Colin passed away almost six years ago now. You would have been very young at the time. How exactly did you know him?" she asked.

Ruth and Joe stepped further into the bus, where the heady smell of fragrance hung in the air.

"I really am very sorry for your loss, Mrs Hartest. I think this will explain everything," Joe said, handing over the letter written to his dad all those years ago.

Mrs Hartest's eyes brightened as she read it. She stroked the curved handwriting with a fingertip and smiled. She looked up. "It's nice to see my Colin's writing again. And you are from Rook Farm?"

Joe nodded.

"All these years I've wondered where Colin hid the pepper pot and ladles. Are you telling me *you* know where they are buried?" She placed the letter on the counter and clasped her hands together, her face brimming with hope.

"Um," said Joe, looking at his shoes.

"Well," said Ruth, her stomach rolling.

Mrs Hartest's neat eyebrows pulled together. "Oh

dear. I sense I won't like what you're about to tell me."

There was a long pause and Ruth shuffled a little closer to Joe until their shoulders were touching.

Joe swallowed and rubbed at his chin. "I'm afraid most of the treasure has been stolen," he said regretfully. The tips of his ears pinked.

Mrs Hartest pressed her hands to her cheeks and blinked. She blinked again. "But…Colin said those items would be safe buried in the ground during the war. How did it happen?"

"It's a long story," said Ruth with a grimace, quickly telling Mrs Hartest about taking the telephone call in Mr Knight's office at the British Museum and her mum coming to Rook Farm to investigate the pepper pot Joe's mum had discovered while ploughing. She spoke about the other ladles that had been found and the night of the break-in. "It's all gone very wrong and we're so dreadfully sorry," she said.

The light in Mrs Hartest's eyes dimmed. "Colin found those objects while volunteering on an archaeological dig not far from here. He was working late and alone one evening and didn't tell anyone what he'd found – not even the landowner. He brought the ladles and pepper pot home with him. I told him it was wrong, and he should do things the right way and report them to the landowner and the Ministry of Works."

"But he didn't because of the war," said Ruth, glancing at Mr Hartest's letter on the countertop, thankful they'd learned the truth about the treasure's origins.

"That's right. Colin thought the pepper pot and ladles were important and decided it was better to hide them. He feared if they went on display in a museum they could get damaged in a bombing raid, or even stolen if we were invaded. After the war he was intending to report them – please believe that. He only did this because of his love of preserving the past. There was no other motive."

Ruth felt terrible. What were they to do?

"I spent so many hours studying my Colin's notebook hoping to learn where the treasure had been buried as well," said Mrs Hartest, her cheeks reddening.

"His notebook!" said Joe, glancing at Ruth.

"You mean…Mr Hartest's field notebook?" said Ruth, her brain buzzing.

"Why, yes," said Mrs Hartest, her fingers worrying at one of her earrings. "It was in Colin's coat pocket when they found him." She shook her head at the tragic memory. "There were pages missing of course. I could never make head nor tail of his scribblings, but I keep it in my handbag. It's silly, but it makes me feel closer to him."

"Do you think…we might take a look at it?" asked Joe hesitantly.

Mrs Hartest stared at them for a few seconds. Then she walked behind the counter and picked up a faded black leather bag with a silver clasp. Opening it, she pulled out a small, tattered blue book. "You can look at it, but I doubt you'll find anything useful."

Joe approached Mrs Hartest. His eyes were glassy. "Thank you, Mrs Hartest. I'm truly sorry for what's happened, but there's a small chance this notebook might lead us to the other finds on our farm that are mentioned in the letter."

Mrs Hartest leaned back against the counter. "Do you really think so?"

Joe nodded. "Perhaps I could copy out some pages from the book while we're here…if you have a spare scrap of paper? You see, our farm is in a bad way; we may even be evicted next week. If we find something buried on the land, we may be able to stop that from happening." He paused and swallowed. "I'm sorry the pepper pot and ladles weren't kept safe on our farm."

Mrs Hartest sighed. She reached forward and patted Joe on the arm. "Now look here. What's done is done. Don't you go blaming yourself." Giving the notebook the same type of lingering look you might to an old friend when saying farewell, she pressed it into his hands. "Take the notebook back to your farm and see if you can decipher Colin's notes. It sounds as if you and your family have had a bad run of luck too. I always say a little kindness goes a long way these days. I would like it returned when you've finished with it though."

"Really? Thank you," said Joe earnestly. "My uncle is going to ask around and see if he can find out who might have stolen the treasure. If we learn anything, we'll be sure to let you know."

"Did you tell the police about the break-in?" asked Mrs Hartest, her forehead creasing.

"Well, no," admitted Ruth.

"If they do learn of it, I wouldn't want poor Colin's name dragged through the mud for what he did. His intentions were wholly honourable," said Mrs Hartest. "It certainly sounds as if the thief knew what they were after when they stole the treasure. Colin used to say there was a thriving black market for Roman artefacts. I imagine that situation has only worsened since the war. So many people are struggling for work and money. They will do anything to survive."

Mrs Hartest's mention of the black market pushed into Ruth's head an image of the petrol containers Terry was hiding in the barn at Rook Farm. The back of her neck began to feel hot and prickly. Terry's business was suffering, and he was short of money. She bit hard on her lower lip as Joe and Mrs Hartest continued to talk. Would Terry's lack of money be a strong enough motive for him to have stolen the treasure? He knew it had been kept in the dresser cupboard. But she had jumped to conclusions before, thinking Lenny and Uncle Gordon had been involved in the theft and she'd been proved badly wrong. Be that as it may, she needed to mention her worries to Joe on the way home and see what he thought about this theory.

CHAPTER 31

Suspicion

"Terry wouldn't have stolen the treasure," said Joe firmly, as their bus wound its way back to Ely and the farm. He glanced up from Mr Hartest's notebook, which he had been poring over since leaving Norwich. "He's not capable of doing anything like that. He's been like a brother to me since Billy left and Dad died. He wouldn't do anything to hurt us."

"But he's hiding black-market petrol in your barn," whispered Ruth. "If the police found out your mum would get in hot water. That's not very fair."

"He was desperate," said Joe. "Mum knew what he

was doing. She just wanted to help him out."

"Being desperate can make people do desperate things," Ruth said, thinking of the looting that had taken place in London when shops had been bombed out during the war. She remembered being especially horrified when her mum had spoken of a few opportunistic wardens and firemen stealing jewellery from the homes of people whose houses had been destroyed. The government had brought in strict criminal sentencing because of the looting.

Joe shook his head. "You're running ahead of yourself, just like you did when you thought Uncle Gordon and Lenny had something to do with the break-in."

Ruth considered his words. She certainly didn't want to make false accusations and had learned from that mistake, but this felt a little different. "Your farm is isolated and so few people knew where the treasure was hidden. The thief knew though. That leaves Terry or Audrey as the only suspects. And Audrey was with us upstairs when the thief broke in, which rules her out."

Joe grimaced. "Suspects? You're speaking like you think you're a detective again."

"But being detectives is the only way we are going to solve this mystery!" exclaimed Ruth, perhaps a little too loudly, for the woman in front turned and gave her a stern tut.

Joe shook his head again, turning his attention back to the notebook.

Ruth slumped back in her seat and folded her arms. She could see why Joe had his doubts. Terry seemed kind and clearly adored Audrey. But he was also struggling for money and had few prospects. Maybe the treasure was a temptation he couldn't turn away from. The only way Joe would believe her was if she found some firm proof.

"Hey, look at this," Joe said after a while, pointing to a yellowing page in the notebook.

Ruth pushed away her troubling thoughts about Terry and leaned over to look. There was nothing recognizable about the faint pencil lines and numbers on the page and she shrugged.

"Look harder," urged Joe. "What do you think this square is?"

"It's just a square," said Ruth, not seeing anything at all.

Joe traced a finger round the square. "I think it's Rook Farm. This is the house and the lines behind it mark the fields and ditches. There's Marsh Field, House

Field, Rook Field, Magpie Field, Gull Field and Eel Field."

Ruth looked harder at the tiny numbers written between two of the lines. "Yes, I see it now!" Mr Hartest had drawn a small circle in Eel Field. Next to the circle were two numbers. 65PSW and 42PE. She drew in a breath. "I know what they mean. They're the number of paces taken south-west and the number of paces taken east from the field boundaries to the excavation. My mum records the locations of finds in the same way."

"A real-life treasure map! The circle marks the spot in Eel Field where Dad found the beads and spearhead," whispered Joe with a sudden laugh. "We can give this map to your mum and Mr Knight tomorrow, Ruth. This is just what we hoped for." He glanced at Ruth. "What is it? You've got a funny look in your eyes. What are you thinking?"

Ruth gently eased the notebook from Joe's hands, her brain whirring as she studied it. Mr Knight would be upset the Roman treasure had been stolen. He would be cross with her mum and unlikely to listen to two children claiming they had found a notebook leading to buried treasure. Even to her ears it sounded a little fantastical, something dreamed up and written about in a story. They could of course show him the spearhead and beads, but Ruth had no idea how significant those finds were. But if she and Joe presented him with evidence of another find...something bigger... that would be a different matter altogether. He would have to take them seriously then. Her chest squeezed at the thought of the harsh words Mr Knight had flung at her the previous summer on the dig. *Children are clumsy and make mistakes.* Her jaw clenched. This was her opportunity to prove him wrong. "If we follow the map and have a careful dig early tomorrow at first light, we might find something beside the spearhead and beads... something that will impress Mr Knight, make him listen and take action to help your farm. It will also help my mum," she said.

Joe's eyes widened. "But that's barmy! Mr Hartest told my dad not to dig around in case anything got damaged. We need a proper archaeologist to help." He looked again at the notebook in Ruth's hand. "I don't want to make a mistake. Too much has gone wrong already."

"And that's exactly why we have to do this," said Ruth. "I know what to do, Joe. I'll make sure this goes right."

CHAPTER 32

The Van

Dash's gruff barks greeted Ruth and Joe as they approached the farmhouse. Dusk had fallen quickly, and Ruth's toes were numb after the long walk up the track from the bus stop.

"I hope my mum is starting to feel better. She'll hate being away from the farm," said Joe, as an owl floated above the ditch. Its broad wings appeared almost weightless in the air before it dived, hunting for prey.

"Maybe Terry has an update from the hospital," said Ruth, seeing his van in the yard. She looked to the barn where the petrol was hidden. If Terry had been involved in the theft of the pepper pot and ladles she needed to find some proof. Perhaps the barn was as good a place as any to start looking for it.

Audrey peered into the scullery as they opened the door; her cheeks flushed. "Where in heaven's name have you been, Joe?" she asked, wiping her hands on her apron. "You can't just leave a note about an urgent task and disappear with Ruth for the day. I've been imagining all sorts."

"We've been to Norwich," said Joe, truthfully, pulling off his shoes.

Audrey blinked and her hands dropped to her side. "Why?"

"I can't say," said Joe, giving Ruth a quick look.

Audrey shook her head in exasperation. "Why not?"

Joe pressed his lips together and Ruth concentrated hard on taking off her outdoor clothes, feeling guilty for the worry they had caused.

"You're keeping secrets. I don't like this," Audrey said thinly.

Ruth's cheeks burned and she felt Audrey's eyes settle on her inquisitively.

"Does Terry have any news of Mum?" Joe asked, quickly changing the subject as he ruffled Dash's neck.

"She's improving slowly," said Audrey, who had turned her attention to her bracelet and was stroking the curves and dips of each charm. "Terry dropped off some things for her at the hospital. He even took her some chocolates. It was a nice thought, but I don't like him spending his money like that."

Ruth's eyebrows tugged together as she followed Audrey and Joe into the kitchen, where the smell of roasting meat hung in the air.

Terry sat in the rocking chair reading a newspaper. "The wanderers return," he said. His voice was a little tight and he gave Audrey a pointed look, perhaps wanting her to scold them a little more forcefully. But she was distracted now, busy stirring a pot on the range.

Ruth stared at Terry. How had he managed to buy chocolates for Mary when he was so short of money? She felt in her coat pocket for her gloves, an idea growing. She glanced at the window overlooking the yard. The curtains were drawn to. "I think I dropped a glove outside. I'll just go and see if I can find it," she said.

"Don't be long. I'm dishing up tea soon," said Audrey. "Take a torch. It's dark out."

Ruth took a torch from the scullery and opened the door. The thin beam of light wobbled as she strode round the edge of the house to the yard. She glanced at the kitchen window and the gentle glow of light behind the curtains. No one was watching, but she needed to be quick.

A fat snowflake fluttered across the beam of her torch, then another. She pressed on across the yard, passing Terry's van. She looked once more at the house, but all was quiet and still. Striding into the barn, she wound her way past tools, buckets and past some hay bales stacked against one wall. Finding the spot behind the tractor where Terry had hidden the petrol, Ruth pulled back the canvas sheeting that covered the containers. She flashed the torch over them in a slow arc, the blue metal glinting. Crouching down, she searched behind and in between the containers for the small hessian bundle containing the ladles and pepper pot. But there was nothing there. She let out a small, frustrated sigh.

Retracing her steps, Ruth was about to return to the house when she glanced at Terry's van. She paused, running over in her mind the events of the previous morning. Terry had come over with a piece of wood to mend the scullery door. Joe had offered to fetch the wood from his van, but Terry had stopped him. Was there an innocent explanation for that, or had there been something in the van Terry hadn't wanted Joe to see? They had no other leads as to who had taken the treasure. Terry really was the only suspect left.

The curtains at the kitchen window were still; no one was looking for Ruth yet. She stood staring at the van for a few seconds more. It was one thing to search the barn, but quite another to look in Terry's van without his permission. But her need for proof to solve the mystery of the stolen treasure was making the tips of her fingers tingle.

Holding her breath, she reached for the van's rear door handle and opened it with a small clunk. It was heavy and she struggled to push it back. Holding the torch under her left arm, she tugged on the handle with both hands. It sprang open and she stumbled backwards. Her torch dropped to the ground with a thud, rolling between the back wheels and underside of the van. It shot staccato flickers around the yard and then went out.

The sudden darkness was oppressive. Ruth heard Dash give a gruff bark from inside the house. Had they heard the torch drop from inside the house? She felt a flurry of snowflakes press on her cheeks like the lightest of fingertips. She shivered, hearing a scrabbling noise to her left by the barn. Peering into the dark, her hands slowly balled into fists. *Was someone watching?* She stifled a yelp as something small and lightning-swift darted close to her toes. It was just a rodent. A rat or a mouse. She had become immune to their scuttles and squeaks while sheltering in the Underground.

Gathering her breath, Ruth turned her attention back to the vehicle. Without the torch she would struggle to search it. Reaching inside, she ran her fingers over planks of wood, several metal buckets, and the stiff muddy bristles of a broom. Quickly pulling out the broom, she used it to retrieve the torch from beneath the van. She flicked it on and off. There was no light. The bump to the ground had broken it.

With a sigh of frustration, she placed it by her feet and clambered inside the van. She crawled blindly across the planks, her fingers searching for anything suspicious. Her trousers snagged on a splinter and she twisted the fabric to wiggle her way free. Near the front of the vehicle, she brushed past a roll of canvas. Her fingers felt something rather unexpected behind it.

Something smooth and silky. She carefully lifted the item up and saw it was a gift bag with ribbon handles.

Climbing out of the van, she held the bag up to what little light there was. She ran her fingers over the bumpy lettering. *Cellini's Jewellers*. Tentatively reaching inside, she pulled out a small box. Flipping open the lid she smothered a gasp. A ring with a gemstone glinted in the dark. But Audrey had said Terry couldn't afford to buy her an engagement ring. This really was very suspicious – how had he got the money for this, and all the other things he'd been buying?

CHAPTER 33

This is the Spot

Ruth's appetite had been whisked away with the discovery of the ring in Terry's van. She pushed the roast duck around her plate until Audrey looked at her with concern and asked if she was sickening for something. "No. I'm fine. Really," she replied. She glanced at Terry who had eaten quickly and was now reading the newspaper again at the table. "Do you want a big wedding?" she asked. Ruth hadn't had the opportunity to tell Joe about her discovery and he gave her a puzzled look.

"I do…well I did," said Terry from behind his paper.

Audrey threw him an unhappy look. There was a tension in his words that Ruth was struggling to interpret. Had Terry and Audrey had an argument?

"We don't need a big wedding. I'll be happy just to be married," said Audrey. She picked a piece of duck from her plate and held it out to Dash. He gobbled it up and licked his lips. "Good boy," she whispered, fondling his ears.

Terry lowered the paper, his lips pulled into a thin line. "You know how I feel about things, Audrey. I…"

"Stop it, Terry." Audrey's words were as sharp as a knife. She pushed back her chair and carried the dirty plates to the scullery without another word.

"Is everything all right?" asked Joe, holding his fork in mid-air.

Terry didn't respond. Clearing his throat, he shook the paper out and carried on reading.

"But how would you pay for a big wedding?" asked Ruth, unable to keep the words inside. From the corner of her eye, Ruth saw Joe's puzzled expression had turned into one of dismay. He gave her a small shake of his head. She decided not to meet her friend's eyes in case the boldness she was feeling disappeared.

"You're asking a lot of questions," Terry said with a frown.

Ruth held Terry's gaze. "We've had to cut back on nice things at home. I imagine it's hard for you to find money too."

Terry glanced towards the scullery. His face suddenly looked hollow and very tired. It was quiet in there and Ruth wondered if Audrey was listening.

Joe threw Ruth another pointed look. She needed to stop this now, before she went too far. Ruth pushed her chair back. "I'm tired. I think I might go to bed."

Terry folded his paper slowly. "I think I'll head off home too. It's been a long day." He glanced again at the scullery where the sound of running water and clatter of dishes could now be heard.

Ruth had found no evidence that Terry had stolen the pepper pot and ladles, but there was still something suspicious about his behaviour. On the one hand he complained about his business suffering, yet on the other he found the money to buy Audrey and Mary gifts. It was like a mathematics equation that she didn't have the answer for and time was running out to find it.

The next morning, Joe knocked quietly on Ruth's door before the sun had risen. She flicked on her torch and quickly got ready, pulling on a jumper, her trousers and two pairs of socks. As she crept downstairs, she wondered if it was ridiculous to assume that, in the space of a few hours, they would successfully use Mr Hartest's notebook to find something so important that Mr Knight's mouth would form a wide O of surprise and delight. It had taken the archaeologists working on the Kent dig a few days to make their first discovery. A hard lump of worry lodged in her throat.

Ruth found Joe in the kitchen stirring a pot of porridge while Dash contentedly gnawed a bone on his rug.

"We'll need to keep our strength up. The snow might not have settled last night, but the air feels heavy today. Any snow that falls will set firm," said Joe.

Ruth glanced out of the window into the dark. Of course she wanted her mum and Mr Knight to arrive safely, but if the poor weather extended their journey, she and Joe would have a little more time to excavate. But then, any snow would also make digging a much tougher task.

After a hurried breakfast, they set off across the fields.

The rucksack of tools bounced uncomfortably against Ruth's spine as she walked, a bucket swinging like a clock pendulum in one hand, her torch in the other.

"I've been thinking about that ring you found in Terry's van," said Joe after a while. The two shovels he'd brought clanked as he trudged on.

Ruth glanced at her friend. It was too dark to see his expression properly. She had told him about searching the barn and Terry's van just before going to bed the previous evening. He had been surprised to hear about the ring and had no answer for how Terry could have paid for it.

"Dash didn't follow me into the fog the night of the break-in," Joe said. "He barked when the thief smashed the glass in the scullery door, but perhaps he wasn't as stirred up as he would have been if a stranger had done it."

"But that still isn't firm proof Terry took the treasure," said Ruth with a frown.

"No. It isn't," said Joe. "But what you said is right. Only Terry and Audrey – or someone they might have told – knew where the treasure was hidden. I agree Audrey couldn't have been involved. But I need to ask Terry about it."

Ruth glanced at Joe's jutting jaw. He was becoming

less cautious, actively seeking answers to his problems and that was a good thing.

"Oh, did you give Audrey the photograph from Hilda at the tearoom yesterday?" asked Ruth, thinking of the two happy girls doing handstands in front of the villa, and their strange discovery that Audrey spent her days off at the tearoom.

Joe's face fell and he patted his coat pocket. "I clean forgot. I'll give it to her later."

As they crossed into Rook Field, they passed the two trenches Ruth's mum had dug. Doubts began to crowd in on Ruth again. She had paid attention to her mum's excavation techniques, knew how to mark out a site and use a trowel, but could she and Joe really do this on their own? She was only twelve. What if she accidentally damaged something or made a mistake?

The water-filled ditch marking the boundary to Magpie Field was half frozen, the fragile ice reminding Ruth of the thin brandy snaps she and her mum occasionally made with their precious sugar and treacle rations. "I've never known my mum to work in conditions as cold as this," she said, as they crossed the bridge. She felt a burn of worry. What if the soil was too hard to break?

"We'll have to do the best we can. Come on, another two fields and we'll be there," said Joe firmly.

"I don't know about this, Joe," said Ruth, coming to a halt. They were close to Lenny's hut in Magpie Field now, the smell of woodsmoke drifting through the air.

Joe turned. His nose was pink and running, but his eyes glimmered in the growing light. "We have to do this for my mum and yours."

The purplish dawn was gradually being consumed by hungry grey clouds scudding in from the east. A snowflake landed on Ruth's eyelash, and she blinked it away, thinking of her mum's wish for a job at the museum, her dad's mural and the memories she was so desperately trying to hang on to. "But what if something does go wrong?"

Joe smiled. Leaning the shovels against his legs, he reached forward and grasped Ruth's hand tight, wringing the doubt from her fingers. "There's always a chance things will go wrong. But there's also a chance things will go right. We'll never know unless we try."

Ruth squeezed his hand back, then straightened her shoulders and smiled. "You're good at giving advice."

Joe's smile broadened into a grin. "Almost as good as you."

Ruth rolled her eyes and they walked on, silvery flakes of snow falling more steadily now, settling into the nooks and crannies of the rutted fields. By the time they reached the hedged boundary of Eel Field, Joe's cap was tipped with white, like a cake dusted with icing sugar.

"We'd better hurry," said Joe, glancing up. "When blizzards roll in, the land is so flat sometimes you can't tell your left from your right. It's easy to get lost." Placing the shovels down by the gnarly hedge, he pulled Mr Hartest's notebook from his pocket and opened it to the plan of the farm. Ruth shone her torch on the page. "Sixty-five paces south-west and forty-two paces east."

Joe looked up. "The sun rises in that direction so that's east. This is the spot we need to start from to head south-west," he said, pointing along the hedgerow boundary. "You count in your head, and I'll count in mine."

Ruth adjusted the rucksack and took a deep breath. She turned and began to count.

Joe picked up the shovels and called for Ruth to stop. "The steps we're taking are too small. My dad had a big stride. We need to try and match it, or we'll end up in the wrong place."

"Of course," said Ruth, berating herself for missing this important point herself.

They turned round and quickly walked back to the starting point.

Joe set off again, his steps larger this time.

Ruth followed, counting silently in her head.

Joe eventually stopped. "Sixty-five steps," he said, his breath pluming.

"I made it sixty-three," said Ruth with dismay.

"Oh," said Joe, looking uncertain. "But I'm sure I counted right."

Ruth pulled her scarf down and drew in a breath of stinging air. "But you're not totally sure?"

Joe chewed on his bottom lip.

"If you did miscount by two steps, we might start digging in the wrong place," said Ruth.

"But what if *you* were wrong?" said Joe.

"We'll have to go back and count again," said Ruth, with a rising frustration. This was just what she had been afraid of. If they made a mess of things now, they could fail before they'd even begun.

Joe nodded his agreement and they trudged back to the starting point. "Ready?" he sighed.

Ruth nodded and they walked and counted again,

this time coming to a halt in the exact same spot. They both grinned.

"Now we need to head east for forty-two paces," said Ruth. The field was flat and unremarkable, but it was also planted with sugar beet, their leafy green fronds sparkling with the rapidly settling snow. She noticed they were now walking directly towards a water-filled channel, almost as wide as a river.

They stepped between the beets, dodging from left to right in an awkward dance. Snow dust streamed above the ground and the sound of pulsing water grew louder.

They came to a stop at the same time.

"This is the spot," said Joe, his eyebrows pulling together. "It doesn't look this close to the channel on the map."

Ruth stared, shining her torch all around. Was this the right spot? This was not like the flat field where the ladles had been found, or the mound site in Kent she had been so keen to have a go at excavating. They had walked beyond the sugar beet and were standing on a low slope a few feet from the edge of the channel. Ruth strode the last few steps up the bank and saw two ducks waddling and skidding on the ice forming at the edges of the expanse of water, quacking quietly to one another.

"What now?" asked Joe.

Ruth summoned all her confidence and pulled her gloves on tightly. They had to trust they were in the right place and get started. "We begin to dig."

CHAPTER 34

Blizzard

"How deep do we need to dig?" asked Joe, handing Ruth a shovel as he stood looking at the slope beside the channel.

Ruth took the shovel from him and shrugged off the rucksack, brushing away the settling snow. "Did your dad find the glass beads and spearhead when he was ploughing?" she said, pulling out two trowels from the rucksack and placing them on the ground.

Joe looked back at the field of beets, which stopped a few feet from where they were standing. He slowly shook his head. "I don't remember him ever saying it like that. In any case, he wouldn't have ploughed up here. He might have been up here inspecting the water levels though. Dad always said this is one of the widest and oldest channels on the farm."

Ruth nodded and bent to examine the soil. Under the settling snow lay patchy scrub. "Let's peg out a square on the slope and dig with the shovels. Then we can use the trowels to search more carefully. I'll draw a quick plan of the site before we start."

Ruth's hands ached with the effort of digging out the square of hard ground they had marked with pegs and twine. Thick, fat snowflakes continued to settle and she sniffed repeatedly to stop her nose from running.

Joe mirrored her actions, his eyes watering as the relentless wind blew and the rising sun bathed them in an eerie glow.

Ruth glanced around at the white and unfamiliar world she now found herself in. The field boundaries were blurry and indistinct. Joe was right: the sky and the ground were fast merging into one enormous swathe of nothingness. Her mum excavated in most weathers, but Ruth felt even she would have been defeated by this. Still, they could not give up. They had come too far and there was too much at stake.

Joe had chipped away a shallow trench the length of his forearm. Under a thin layer of hard topsoil lay wet peat and silt; it would take them weeks if they continued at this slow pace. Ruth wondered what her mum would have advised. She remembered her patient but determined hands digging and scraping the soil, her eyes hunting for artefacts that were often elusive, as if unwilling to give up their hiding places. "Slow and steady wins the race," her mum would say. There was no cutting of corners in archaeology. She needed to be thorough, methodical, and clear-headed.

Ruth dug on, snow flurries blurring her vision, her palms stinging as blisters formed under her gloves. The mound of excavated soil grew higher and after the pearly white sun had finally risen, her shovel clinked the top of something hard. She crouched down to look. "Joe," she called, her words whipped by the wind.

Joe hurried over. "What have you found?"

Using a trowel, Ruth carefully scraped away the peat. The object her shovel had struck was wooden and carved at the tip, as if it had been shaped by an axe. It was the top of a post.

"What's that doing there?" asked Joe, wiping away

some of the thick silt. The wood was crumbly, and a piece broke off in his hand.

Ruth scanned the bottom of the trench and saw a darker patch to the right of the wood. Taking her trowel, she carefully scraped away the mud to expose the carved end of another post.

"Why would these posts have been put here?" asked Joe, his forehead creasing.

"The wood looks old," said Ruth, seeing another dark patch a little further along the trench. These posts were in a line. They hadn't been placed here by accident. She took a deep breath and thought about what her mum had said when they were on the train coming to Rook Farm. *"It's the setting and landscape that give us the real clues to the past, often more than the objects you'll find buried in the soil."*

Ruth stood up, the blood rushing to her head. "We need to keep digging, Joe. Maybe these posts were put here by people who lived here a long time ago. Maybe they are part of a settlement…a building even. That could be why your dad found the beads and spearhead here."

"But how long do we have? Your mum and Mr Knight might arrive soon," said Joe, glancing back in the direction of the house as if he almost expected them to be striding across the fields towards them.

Ruth pushed back her coat sleeve and glanced at her watch. It was eight o'clock. They had been outside for almost two hours. They had excavated quite a pile of soil but found nothing aside from the posts. She had to find something else, something big, before Mr Knight and her mum arrived. "I know there are other things here, we just need to keep searching," she said, using the tape measure to work out the distance between the posts and recording the locations on the plan she had drawn.

Joe must have seen the fresh determination in her eyes, as he gave a brisk nod. "Where do we dig next?"

"Right here, round the posts," she replied, pushing the paper and pencil back into her coat pocket. Ruth excavated round the second post, which lay closer to the edge of the channel, the water and ice glistening below her. If she lost her footing and fell backwards, she could easily slip into the water. The thought made her plant her boots more firmly into the trench.

"Ruth...come and see this," called Joe from where he was standing by the first post. His voice was high and excited. She saw he was holding a small object in the air. The weak light glinted off it. *It was metallic.*

Ruth stepped over to Joe and kneeled beside him, the silt and snow seeping through her already muddy trousers and chilling her skin. "Here, let me see." She examined the object he had found, her heart leaping. "It looks like an axe head. See this hole in one end? Perhaps this was used to attach it to a handle, just like the spearhead your dad found."

"There are more things here too," Joe said excitedly, gesturing to the mound of soil he had just excavated.

Ruth searched through the soil with the tip of her trowel. A blue glint caught her eye, then another, then another. She carefully pulled them out.

"More glass beads," exclaimed Joe, bending over to look, as the snow drifted down more thickly.

"Keep excavating – but only use the trowel. We don't want to damage anything we find," said Ruth, her own excitement mounting. She pushed the beads into her coat pocket and added their location to the site plan, which was becoming horribly muddy and damp, her pencil puncturing the paper in places. Turning her attention back to the soil, she forgot all about the cold pinching her toes and stinging her cheeks as she surveyed the dig.

"I've found another axe head," called Joe in wonder a short while later.

Ruth grinned and scraped repeatedly at the soil with her own trowel, thinking about Mary's hospital bill and the need to save the farm, and then about her mum and Mr Knight. The things they were finding might solve all their problems. Her trowel clinked and she paused. It didn't sound like wood this time. It sounded like metal. Had she found an axe head too? Placing her trowel to one side, she brushed away the falling snow. Feeling a wave of dizziness, she took a deep breath. Her gloves were soaking wet, the knitted wool heavy and stiff. Peeling them off, she began to feel around in the soil with her fingertips. Then she saw it. A dull, brown corkscrew of metal. With trembling hands, Ruth gently pulled the object out and wiped away the remaining mud with her glove. The dullness quickly faded, revealing something that made her breath catch in her throat. She blinked. Blinked again. The thin and rigid corkscrew of metal was shaped like a necklace with an opening at one end. And it was yellow. *Gold?*

Closing her eyes for a few seconds, she mentally trod through the halls of the British Museum, trying to recall anything she had seen that was similar. But all she could picture were schoolchildren swarming around the Egyptian mummies, chattering loudly in their excitement.

"What have you found there?" said a voice to her right.

Ruth flicked her eyes open and turned, her numb fingers almost dropping the necklace into the trench.

Terry stood a short distance away, snowflakes swirling like agitated moths round his head.

Ruth swallowed her fear and stood up. He had crept up on them silently in the snow.

Joe ran over, three axe heads clutched in his hands. "Terry. What are you doing out here?"

Terry took a step forward and wiped the snow from his cheeks. "You're digging for more treasure?" His eyes widened as he took in the axe heads and the necklace.

Joe was staring at the necklace too. "Is that...gold?" he asked, his voice high.

"You've just dug these things up? Can I see?" Terry took a step closer and held out his hands.

Ruth and Joe shared an uncertain look.

"I think...I think I should take the things you've found. I can keep them safe for you," said Terry quickly. His eyes were glassy, his lips trembling.

"No," said Ruth, wishing her voice wasn't quite so cracked and small.

Terry blinked, took a step forward and stretched out his gloved fingers, reaching for the gleaming gold.

"No...you can't have any of these things," said Joe fiercely, taking a step backwards and slipping the axe heads into his coat pockets.

Joe's sudden movement caused Terry to stumble, and he fell clumsily to his knees.

Ruth's legs buzzed as if electricity was flowing through her veins. *They must keep the things they had found safe and hand them over to her mum and Mr Knight.* "We need to get back to the house," she said in a low voice, quickly and carefully pushing the necklace into her coat pocket.

"You go now. I'll follow," replied Joe through gritted teeth, taking another step back from Terry, who was standing up and brushing slushy mud from his trousers. Terry's chest was puffed up and he looked as if was about to blow his top.

Ruth gave her friend one last look, then turned on her heels and fled.

CHAPTER 35

Proof

Ruth's boots pounded over the snowy field, away from the excavation site and Terry. She stumbled over a beet and, gritting her teeth, began placing her feet more carefully. She felt for the gold necklace and the beads in her pocket. They could be significant historical finds. It was vital she handed them over to her mum and Mr Knight.

Joe quickly caught up, the axe heads chinking in his pockets as he ran. His mouth was set firm. "Terry must have stolen the treasure – you saw how he wanted the other things we've found."

"Fancy using the excuse that he wanted to keep them safe!" Ruth panted, her lungs burning. The falling snow was disorienting, and she fought to control waves of dizziness and an overwhelming urge to pause and gain her bearings.

"We'll have to let the police know," puffed Joe, his eyes darkening.

Ruth glanced behind to see if Terry was following. She didn't believe he would hurt them, but if he saw an opportunity to take the items, he might decide to pursue them.

Joe surged on, his feet thudding over the dips in the field as he disappeared into a fresh swirl of snow.

A burst of determination forced Ruth's feet forward, her leg muscles screaming as she streaked behind him across the field. A sudden rise in the land brought her to a juddering halt. It was the boundary to Eel Field. Her legs trembled and her pulse thudded in her head as she listened for Joe. The wind whizzed around her ears. Had Joe turned left or right? Her eyes roved the ground until she saw his footprints being swallowed up by white. She wanted to call out and beg Joe to wait. But that might alert Terry to where she was. Her teeth chattered and she tried to force down the panic blooming in her chest as she ran along the hedge looking for the opening into Gull Field, her feet slipping and sliding. They had left the excavation site uncovered. Perhaps Terry was rooting around, searching for more treasure.

The blizzard buffeted her from all angles, making her feel as if she were inside a shaken snow globe. She should have stuck closer to Joe and not let him out of her sight. She blinked back frustrated tears.

Her boots slipped and she tripped forward, hitting her shoulder on the hard ground. The snow continued to surge as she fought to catch her breath, the hiss of the wind wild in her ears.

The pound of feet was sudden, as were the gentle hands grabbing her arm and helping her to her feet.

"Joe," Ruth breathed in relief.

"I thought you were behind me," Joe said, warm air heaving from his lips. "I turned and you were gone. I don't think Terry's following us," he said, glancing back into the blizzard as they slipped through the gap in the hedge and ran on through Gull Field.

There was a small break in the clouds and Ruth's eyes burned with hot tears of relief as she saw the lights of the farmhouse in the far distance guiding them home.

They picked up their pace, Joe sticking close to Ruth's side as they eventually passed the two trenches in Rook Field where the pepper pot and ladles had been found. Ruth looked behind, but there was still no sign of Terry.

As they approached the rear of the house, Ruth saw three figures standing at the scullery window and heard Dash's barked greeting.

"Look. It's your mum and Audrey," called Joe, racing ahead.

"And Mr Knight," breathed Ruth, her chest constricting further.

Ruth saw that Audrey's arms were folded and she wore an expression as tight as a ball of string. She stumbled into the scullery; Joe close on her heels.

"Wherever have the two of you been?" Ruth's mum said with concern.

Audrey looked at them both, bewildered. "Where did you go? You weren't in the house or the yard. You can't keep on disappearing like this. What's going on?"

Ruth tumbled into her mum's arms, breathing in the smell of peppermint drops. "I'm so glad you're here," she cried, struggling to catch her breath.

"Audrey told us about the break-in and the treasure being stolen. How frightening for you," her mum said, holding Ruth at arm's length. Her eyes were glassy as she brushed the snow from Ruth's damp coat and hat. "But…you're covered in mud. What have you been doing?"

Ruth pulled away. She noticed Mr Knight was looking very keenly at the axe heads Joe had placed on the draining board, as Dash sniffed round his feet.

"The stolen treasure didn't come from the farm. It was reburied," said Ruth, the words tumbling from her mouth.

Mr Knight stilled and looked up.

"It belonged to a man called Mr Hartest," continued Ruth. "He had an agreement with Joe's dad, who had found a spearhead and some glass beads in Eel Field."

"Mr Hartest?" said Mr Knight, throwing a glance at Ruth's mum.

Ruth wondered why he said the man's name with such familiarity.

"Go on," Mr Knight said gruffly, gesturing for Ruth to continue.

Ruth swallowed, suddenly feeling small and uncertain under his gaze. She drew in a breath. "In exchange for

Joe's dad burying the pepper pot and ladles, to keep them safe during the war, Mr Hartest was going to come back and excavate the site where the spearhead and beads had been found. But Mr Hartest died in the Baedeker raids."

Mr Knight nodded, as if Ruth was confirming something he already knew.

"The pepper pot and ladles…aren't from here?" said Audrey in a low voice.

"We went to Norwich yesterday and found Mr Hartest's wife. She gave us his notebook," chimed in Joe, holding it up. "It has a map that led us to the channel in Eel Field."

"You need to come and see, Mum. There are these odd posts sticking out of the mud. Joe found some axe heads and I found these." Ruth reached into her pocket and pulled out the beads and twisted gold necklace, as well as the plan she had made of the site.

Ruth's mum's eyes widened like saucers.

Mr Knight pulled in a sharp breath. "A gold torc," he whispered, drawing closer, like a bee to nectar. He held out a palm. "May I?" he said softly. Ruth nodded and handed over the items and the soggy piece of paper.

"But then Terry arrived," said Ruth.

"We think…he may have stolen the ladles and pepper pot," said Joe, looking at Audrey.

"We ran back here. We needed to keep these new things safe," said Ruth.

Ruth's mum's eyes widened. She looked to Joe and then to Ruth. "You're saying Terry is the thief?"

Audrey's bottom lip quivered, and she wrapped her arms round her middle.

"Well, we don't have any firm proof. But it has to be someone who knew where the treasure was hidden," said Ruth.

Audrey blinked and blinked. Her eyes strayed to the window and the tapping snowflakes.

Above the noise of the whirling wind, the thud of footsteps approached the house. Through the blizzard Ruth saw Terry striding towards the door with a grim intent, his shoulders hunched up to his ears. He looked very angry indeed.

CHAPTER 36

Accusations

The air in the scullery was thick with tension as Terry flung open the door.

Ruth felt a little sick as she watched him pull off his cap and gloves. Snow scattered on the floor and quickly melted. Dash sniffed and licked at it.

"Did you steal the pepper pot and ladles from the house?" Joe asked Terry bluntly, moving to stand beside Audrey.

"Now wait a minute, Joe," said Ruth's mum, stepping forward. "That's a jolly big accusation to make."

Audrey fiddled with her bracelet; her eyes focused on Terry.

"You think I...am the thief?" said Terry, his eyes widening. "Is that why you ran off?" A wave of sadness swept across Terry's face and he glanced at Audrey.

Ruth's mum placed a hand on Joe's arm. "Terry very kindly went to search for you after we arrived and found you were missing. What makes you think he took the pepper pot and ladles?"

Mr Knight was still standing by the draining board. He had laid the necklace and beads beside the axe heads and was looking at Ruth's hastily drawn plan. He slowly shook his head as if he couldn't believe what he was seeing, oblivious to the commotion going on around him.

"Terry has no money, but he's been buying things. I found a ring in the back of his van," began Ruth. "It seemed a bit...suspicious."

Audrey placed a hand to her lips.

A pink rash crept up Terry's neck like a vine. He threw Audrey another anxious glance then looked back at Ruth. "You've been rooting around in my van?"

Ruth's mum raised her eyebrows, and gave Ruth a disappointed look.

Ruth felt suddenly small and a little unsure.

Snow flicked against the scullery windows like grains of rice. Dash whined and rubbed against Joe's legs.

Audrey backed away into the kitchen, her fingers worrying over her charm bracelet, moving from the tiny dancing shoe to the shell and back again.

"The ring in my van was bought with money I borrowed from my mother. It was to be a surprise for Audrey – the engagement ring I wanted to give her but couldn't afford," said Terry. He looked at Audrey, his eyes suddenly soft. "I'm sorry, love. You need to tell them…now."

Turning on her heel, Audrey slipped into the kitchen, her arms still curled round her middle as if she had a sore stomach.

Ruth looked back at Terry. "What does Audrey need to tell us?" she asked.

Terry followed Audrey into the kitchen.

Ruth and Joe exchanged a worried look and trailed after him, Ruth's brain whirring as she tried to gather her scattered thoughts. She heard her mum whispering to Mr Knight, saying it was probably best he stayed in the scullery while she helped deal with the situation.

Audrey stood at the dresser, staring at the cupboard

where the ladles and pepper pot had been hidden.

Terry grasped her hands. "Tell them. No good will come of keeping a secret like this."

Audrey pulled away from Terry, lowered her head and turned to face them all. A tear trickled down one cheek. "Terry had nothing to do with taking the treasure. It was me. I took the pepper pot and ladles."

CHAPTER 37

The Truth

Ruth stared at Audrey in undisguised shock at her confession. She felt every muscle in her body tense as she waited to hear Audrey's explanation.

Joe sucked in a breath of disbelief. "It was you who stole the treasure? Mum gave you a job and a home. And this is how you treat her?"

Audrey blinked as she swiped tears from her face.

Joe turned to Terry. "You knew about this and didn't say anything?"

Terry's cheeks were pinched. "I only found out the truth yesterday when you and Ruth were in Norwich.

Audrey confessed what she had done and said she needed my help. I tried to persuade her to own up. I didn't approve of it at all."

Ruth felt a growing anger. "You broke the glass in the back door, Audrey? You made us believe someone had been in the house? That was rotten," she said, remembering how frightened she had been.

Audrey hung her head. "I didn't mean to cause upset. I truly didn't. There just wasn't…any other way."

"Oh dear. But why do this at all, Audrey?" said Ruth's mum in dismay. "What have you done with the treasure? Did you sell it on?"

Audrey shook her head. "The pepper pot and ladles are in a shoebox in my wardrobe. But yes, I was going to sell them," she said quietly. She glanced at Terry. "Terry knows a man who works on the black market. I told Terry what I'd done and asked if this man might want to buy the treasure. But Terry wasn't having anything to do with it. He said I needed to own up."

A sheen of sweat peppered Terry's hairline and he gave a disappointed shake of his head.

Joe looked at Terry. "In the field just now, I thought you wanted the necklace and axe heads for yourself."

Terry shook his head. "I just wanted to keep them safe," he said.

Audrey's face crumpled in dismay. "I wouldn't have taken them as well. You have to believe me," she said.

Ruth felt a strong sense of relief that all of the treasure was safe but she was bewildered that, despite Audrey's devotion to the Sterne family, she had treated Joe and his family so terribly.

The charms on Audrey's bracelet jangled as she brushed away more tears.

Ruth glanced at the bracelet, thinking about what she and Joe had learned in Hilda's tearoom about Audrey not visiting her family in Norwich each month. She thought of what Lenny had said about seeing Audrey crying in the fields. She swallowed. "Is this something to do with your family, Audrey?"

Audrey turned to Ruth, high spots of colour flaming her cheeks. She swayed a little and Terry quickly pulled out a chair from the table and lowered her into it. Audrey took a steadying breath as she searched for some much-needed courage. "I suppose this is to do with my family," she replied. "But not in the way that you think. They don't need money. I wasn't stealing the treasure for them."

Ruth glanced at the tiny shoe charm that Audrey was so fond of. She was fiddling with it again, turning it over and over as she assembled her thoughts.

"Tell them what you told me yesterday," urged Terry. "It might help them understand."

"Go on," said Joe, his lips thin.

Audrey pulled in a deep breath. "Those early years of the war were hard. Dad worked long hours at the shoe factory in Norwich. Me, Mum and Emma dug an Anderson shelter in the back garden where we'd sit at night when the sirens sounded. In the morning we'd come out of the shelter, frozen and blinking in the light. Emma and I complained to Dad how dreadful it was. He worried for us all terribly. One evening his sister, our Aunt Edith, telephoned. She lived just outside Norwich in a villa on Martineau Lane. She was retiring to the coast and her house was to be sold. When she found out how worried Dad was, she said she'd stop the sale and that we could live in her house until the war was over."

Joe and Ruth exchanged a glance. Joe reached into his coat pocket and pulled out the photograph of Martineau Lane that Hilda had given them at the tearoom. He pushed it across the table.

Audrey picked up the photograph, her fingers trembling. "Where did you get this?"

"When Joe and I went to Norwich yesterday we visited the tearoom you go to in Ely. Hilda said you sit there all day once a month, just reading," said Ruth.

Terry's eyebrows tugged together. "But I drop Audrey at the station every month thinking she's visiting her family!" He stared at Audrey intently. "What's going on, love? Have you been keeping other things from me too?"

A horrible idea wormed its way under Ruth's skin as she thought about the Baedeker Raids in Norwich and the terrible destruction they had caused. She thought of Audrey's sister's name spelled out in delicate silver charms. Audrey had lied about visiting her family but was there a deeper and darker secret she had been hiding from them all? "Did something happen to your family in the war?" she asked quietly.

Ruth's mum pulled out a chair and sat opposite Audrey, her face racked with concern.

Audrey's chin wobbled and she sniffed. "We moved to Martineau Lane. It was surrounded by fields, and you could hear cows and pigs from the back door. We heard the drone of the Luftwaffe, but no bombs fell near us. Dad felt so safe he didn't even build an Anderson shelter in the garden; said we could always shelter in a ditch if the worst happened."

Ruth nibbled on a thumbnail, waiting with trepidation for Audrey to continue.

Joe's eyes were still fixed on Audrey. "I don't see how this is connected to you stealing the ladles and pepper pot," he said.

Audrey looked at the ceiling and took a deep breath. "Norwich suffered two nights of heavy air raids. The skies towards the centre of the city burned bright orange with all the fires. Emma was upset one evening. She couldn't find her charm bracelet. The last time she remembered seeing it was in the Anderson shelter at our old house. The house was still unoccupied, so I caught a bus into the city and went to find it. Emma told me not to go – she said it was too dangerous. But I was stubborn and didn't listen. The bracelet was full of good memories, happy memories. I had to find it."

Ruth placed a hand to her mouth, swallowing a burn of unease.

"The Luftwaffe returned for a third night of bombing. Nobody knows for sure why the bombs fell on Martineau Lane, rather than on the city that night.

Some people thought the lights from flares led the bombers away from the city to the countryside, that they thought it was an airfield they were targeting. But whatever it was, when I returned home with Emma's bracelet there was nothing left. Even the hedgerows had been shredded to ribbons by the shrapnel."

"Are you telling us your family...didn't...survive?" asked Ruth's mum incredulously.

Audrey nodded and pressed her trembling lips together.

"Oh, Audrey," said Ruth, stepping forward and placing a hand on her arm. The memories of bombs dropping in London as she sheltered underground flew into her head. It had been truly terrifying.

Ruth's mum and Joe had both turned quite pale.

Terry bent down and placed a protective arm round Audrey's shoulders, as if trying to shield her from this terrible truth. His drawn cheeks were as white as the snowflakes drifting past the windows.

A tear dripped from the end of Audrey's nose onto the table. It bled into the wood, and she wiped the smudge away with the pad of a thumb.

Ruth passed Audrey her handkerchief. She took it gratefully and twisted it round her fingers. "I was sixteen. I had no family, no home and no possessions, except the clothes I was standing up in." She glanced again at her bracelet. "Aunt Edith was devastated that her family and home had been destroyed. She wanted me to come and live with her. But I couldn't. I didn't want to talk about or remember what had happened. I wanted to push the memories away. I feel close to Emma and the rest of my family when I wear the bracelet, but it also makes my chest ache when I look at it."

Ruth thought of Emma's name charms lying upstairs on Audrey's dressing table, painful memories she had been trying to push away but hold on to at the same time.

"I joined the Land Army and worked at Rook Farm," continued Audrey. "It's so isolated here, almost like living on an island. I felt safe. Mary and Joe and Terry made me feel loved and I cared for them all deeply. I still do. Meeting them…it was like I'd been given a second chance at happiness. I would do anything for them. Anything at all."

Ruth saw Joe's eyes were shining. He wiped them roughly on his sleeve.

Terry pulled in a shuddering breath, his bottom lip wobbling.

"But then, last year, things started to go wrong," said Audrey dully. "Joe's dad died. The bad weather caused crops to fail. The farm was struggling. The bank even issued an eviction order because of an unpaid loan."

Ruth and Joe looked at Audrey in surprise. "How did you know about that?" exclaimed Joe.

"You know about it too?" asked Audrey, looking bewildered.

Joe nodded.

"Oh. The missing letters from the bank. It was you who took them?" Audrey murmured, with a small shake of her head. "A man came to the farm a month ago, when Mary didn't respond to the letters the bank sent. He told us we had until next week to pay back the loan."

"I was hiding the bank letters from Mum. I didn't know what to do," Joe said miserably.

Audrey gave him a sorrowful look. "We were hiding the eviction from you too. Your mum and I didn't want to worry you, Joe. You've had so much to cope with and you've worked so hard to help."

A sad realization dawned on Ruth. "Mary kept on working when she was sick because of the eviction notice, then?"

Audrey nodded and Joe looked stricken.

"But there's something I don't understand. Why take the treasure when you knew I'd come from the museum to help?" asked Ruth's mum, her eyebrows knitting together.

Ruth's eyes widened, the final piece of the puzzle suddenly clicking into place as she thought back to their arrival. "Because when we arrived, Mum, you said it could take months for the museum to decide whether they wanted to buy the treasure. The eviction notice and then Mary going into hospital meant money was needed now."

Audrey stifled a small sob and nodded. "Ruth's right. When Mary went into hospital, I realized I had to do something to save the farm. Taking the treasure and selling it myself seemed the only solution."

Joe frowned. "But why lie to us about your family still being alive?"

Audrey reached up for Terry's hand, and he clasped it tight. "I didn't set out to lie about my family having lost their lives, but it was easier than speaking of it. Don't get me wrong, I cry about it something dreadful when no one is around," she said, lowering her eyes. "But I know I should have told you all the truth. I tried to run away from my past, but I couldn't. It will always be there."

Audrey had done a terrible thing pretending to break in and stealing the treasure, but it hadn't been done with malice. Ruth felt a burn of guilt beneath her ribs for thinking Terry was responsible and searching his van. She needed to make amends for that. At the same time, Ruth understood the desperate measures Audrey had gone to and the secrets she had kept to protect those she loved. Ruth looked at Joe's and Terry's sober faces and wondered if they would ever find it in their hearts to forgive her.

CHAPTER 38

Apologies

Audrey pushed back her chair and stood up, her face blotchy. "I'll fetch you the ladles and pepper pot now." She turned to Joe. "Please tell Mrs Hartest I'm terribly sorry. You can call the police if you like. I'll tell them everything."

"Audrey, wait," said Terry, but she fled from the room, her feet thumping up the stairs.

"Leave her for a moment, Terry," Ruth's mum said, as he made to go after her. "This is a lot for us to take in and perhaps she needs a moment alone."

"I never guessed anything was wrong," said Terry,

returning to the table and sinking into his seat. "She always put on such a bright face, was so determined. I'm as shocked as you to learn the truth about her family, and I'm still reeling from her decision to take the treasure."

"I'm sorry I looked in your van, Terry," said Ruth in a small voice, truly meaning it. "I was so set on finding out who had taken the treasure I made some bad decisions. I really am a rotten detective."

"I'm sorry too," said Joe, giving Ruth a grimace and Terry an apologetic look.

"I can see why you might have thought I had something to do with it, what with me hiding the ring and buying nice things. I should have been honest with you about borrowing money from my mum. It seems all of us have had our secrets," said Terry, wiping his hands over his pallid face. He glanced at Ruth's mum. "Audrey has a good heart. She was wrong to do what she did, but she had good intentions."

Ruth heard Mr Knight clearing his throat at the scullery door. He peered into the kitchen. "Is it all right to come in?" He looked out of place in the farmhouse, dressed in his suit and tie – from another world entirely.

Ruth's mum nodded. "Yes, please do. I am sorry.

Our visit to the farm hasn't turned out quite as I'd planned."

Mr Knight waved a hand dismissively. "I overheard much of the conversation, and it seems the ladles and pepper pot are safe. But I must say, what does excite me is what these children have found." He looked at Joe. "Do you think you might take me to the site where you recovered these things? I believe these objects are very old indeed. An extraordinary find."

Joe's eyes brightened. "It was all Ruth really. She marked out the site and showed me how to use a trowel."

Mr Knight turned his attention to Ruth. His forehead creased. "I remember you were on the Kent dig last summer with your mother. And it was you who took the message on my telephone from Mrs Sterne."

Ruth's cheeks suddenly felt searing hot. She clenched her muddy hands into fists.

To her surprise she saw Mr Knight's lips tilt into an almost-but-not-quite smile. "I don't usually approve of people entering my office without permission, or undertaking digs of their own accord, but in this case your actions have uncovered something quite marvellous."

Ruth's cheeks now felt as if they were on fire. "I am sorry and…um…it was my mum who taught me about archaeology and how to dig."

"She is a good teacher and an asset to the British Museum," said Mr Knight, throwing Ruth's mum a look that made him seem almost approachable. He looked back at Ruth. "Well done, young lady. Your plan of the site is very impressive and if these finds are as important as I think they might be, I imagine the museum will offer to buy them, after they have been valued of course. It seems I must also have a word with the bank about this looming eviction. We can't have them obstructing any further excavations."

Ruth grinned at the look of sheer delight on Joe's face and felt a deep satisfaction that she'd received praise from Mr Knight.

They heard the sound of feet treading carefully down the stairs and a few moments later Audrey appeared with a small brown suitcase and a shoebox wedged under her arm. She placed the case on the floor and held out the box. "I am sorry for what I've done. I've put the few savings I have in here with the treasure. Please use it to pay for the repairs to the broken window," she said to Joe.

Joe took the box and placed it on the kitchen table.

"May I?" asked Mr Knight eagerly, gesturing to the box.

Joe nodded.

Terry stood up, his eyes focused on the suitcase by Audrey's feet. "What's that for, love?"

"You'll be wanting me to leave," began Audrey miserably. "I've packed a few of my things. Maybe you can send the rest of them on once I've found somewhere to live."

Terry's eyes widened and he opened his mouth to speak, but Audrey raised a hand. "Please, Terry. Let me finish." She looked at Mr Knight, who had carefully unwrapped the pepper pot and ladles and placed them on the table, his eyes filling with an undisguised delight.

"I am truly sorry for the lies and the theft. I think when I lost my family, I felt I'd lost a little of my true self too. I was so determined to help Mary and Joe I couldn't see straight. I know it's no excuse, but that's the only way I can explain it," said Audrey.

"We couldn't manage on the farm without your help, Audrey," said Joe softly. "You're part of our family now."

"You…you…don't want me to leave?" asked Audrey, blinking furiously.

"None of us want you to go," said Terry, throwing Joe a thankful look. "I can't say I fully understand what you did, but I've made mistakes too. Now I'm determined to make a success of my business the right way – for both of our futures."

Audrey's cheeks cracked into a small smile. She sniffed, stepped forward and placed a hand on Terry's chest.

"I know Mum's not supposed to have visitors, but could you take me to the hospital and find a way to smuggle me in?" asked Joe. "There's a lot we need to talk about."

"Of course," said Terry. He glanced at the window. The blizzard had abated, the weak sun throwing light onto the snow-dust blowing around the yard. "Looks like the weather forecast wasn't as bad as predicted. The roads should be clear."

Ruth looked away, her eyes suddenly misty. She watched Mr Knight examining the pepper pot and ladles at the kitchen table, a small glow still sitting high in her chest at the memory of the way he'd praised her earlier. She was thankful Joe, Audrey and Terry had admitted their secrets and was sure they would find a way to move on, and that Mr Knight and her mum would do everything they could to stop the eviction. The thought that Joe's farm might be saved made the warm glow inside expand and grow until she felt as if her feet would lift from the floor.

CHAPTER 39

Change

Later that morning, Terry took Joe to visit Mary at the hospital and while Audrey had a much-needed sleep, Ruth and her mum sat at the kitchen table with the treasure finds laid out in front of them on a piece of sacking.

"Gracious. What a time you've had while I was gone," said Ruth's mum, picking up the gold torc and examining it carefully. She then turned her attention to the axe heads. "I've left Mr Knight out there looking at the site. We both think the wooden posts you found could signify some kind of settlement. Houses were built of wood in the Bronze Age and the items you've found would certainly fit in with that period."

Ruth grinned. Her mum had the same glimmer of excitement in her eyes as she'd had when they had arrived four days earlier.

"You did say you can never tell what you might find buried in the ground," said Ruth. Dash nudged her knees and she reached down and fondled his ears. His tail thumped on the tiled floor.

"I see you've found a new friend while I've been gone," said Ruth's mum, glancing under the table with a smile. She looked up. "There are some things I didn't tell you, about why I was so keen to speak with Mr Knight about the Roman silver."

Ruth stared at her mum, eager to hear more.

"You see when I found the ladles, I knew straight away that something wasn't quite right. They were loosely buried in the soil and close to the surface, which suggested they hadn't been there very long. The pepperpot and ladles were also quite polished for items that should have been buried for well over a thousand years. I could see faint abrasive marks, where they had perhaps been cleaned a little too enthusiastically."

Ruth nodded, thinking of how the British Museum

curators had done the very same thing by keeping its treasures hidden below ground during the war, safe from the threat of bombs. "I hope Mrs Hartest won't get into any trouble," she said.

"I am sure the museum and authorities will sympathize with her, but they will need to hear her side of the story," said Ruth's mum. "It will be nice to see the pepper pots and ladles reunited as a set. Mr Knight was very concerned by all of this, of course, which is why he suggested accompanying me today."

It was exciting that the history of the treasure had been uncovered. But what would all this mean for her mum? Mr Knight had said she was an asset. Did that mean he had changed his mind about giving her the job?

As Ruth packed away her clothes in the bedroom upstairs and prepared for the long drive back to London, she glanced outside. The land was silent and still, as if it had been washed white by one of her dad's paintbrushes.

Her mum came into the room and sat on the bed. "Almost ready?"

Ruth nodded, finding it hard to believe that in only a few short hours she would be home.

"Darling. There's something else we need to talk to about."

Ruth looked up.

"I can stay on at the museum as a volunteer, but Mr Knight hasn't changed his mind about the job. You see, he's given the position to someone else," her mum said.

Ruth sat beside her mum and squeezed her hands into fists. "But we'll manage for money, won't we?"

Her mum shook her head. "I'm sorry, Ruth, things have become a bit desperate. Your dad's only just building up his business again and we just can't afford to stay on in our house any more. We have to move."

Tiny dots swam before Ruth's eyes. All this effort to uncover the secrets of the treasure had been for nothing. She let the thought settle. Except it hadn't been for nothing. The secrets she had helped uncover would hopefully save Joe's farm and allow Audrey to come to terms with her sad past.

Ruth watched as her mum picked up the pile of badly folded clothes, placed them in the suitcase and clicked it shut. "I've found a lovely flat, not far from your dad's. You can practically see his living room window from your bedroom."

"I'll miss our house. I miss Dad too," said Ruth, stifling a sob.

Ruth's mum pushed the case to one side, leaned over and folded Ruth into a hug. "You'll see Dad all the time. We will make new memories in our next home. Jolly good ones."

Ruth pulled away from her mum and wiped her eyes. She had encouraged Joe to accept a new future and be positive. She must do the same.

"Your dad and I both love you," said Ruth's mum, kissing her lightly on the head.

Ruth thought about the tiny painted family of three on her bedroom mural. Audrey had lost her home and family. Joe and Mary had desperately tried to hold their farm together, but change was the only way forward. She was proud of her mum's ambition to make a better life for the two of them, and while she might not like the fact her dad was no longer living at home, he had made it through a terrible war unscathed, which was something to be hugely grateful for.

"I love you both too," said Ruth. "Thank you for bringing me with you to Rook Farm. I'll never forget this place."

"I've a feeling we will be back," said her mum with a grin.

Ruth gave her a watery smile in return. Her time at Rook Farm had opened her eyes to a fresh variety of hardships the war had imposed on people. She could not stop time or prevent change, however much she might sometimes like to. But after everything that had happened, they all deserved an optimistic future and she very much hoped they would find it.

CHAPTER 40

Six Months Later

"Look at that," said Joe brightly, as he stood next to Ruth and her mum, staring into the glass display cabinet at the British Museum.

"It is rather amazing," said Ruth with a grin. "What do you think, Audrey?"

Audrey gave a shy smile and stepped forward to read the display card under the glass.

Rook Farm Hoard
The remains of a settlement, discovered at Rook Farm
in the Fens during the winter of 1948, unearthed

some significant artefacts, including bronze axe
heads, swords and spearheads as well as a gold torc.
The finds are estimated to date from the late Bronze
Age and, due to their proximity to a watercourse,
were well preserved in damp conditions. The plant
remains found on the site tell us important cultural
facts about Bronze Age communities and how people
lived, with the remains of wooden hut piles, thatch
and pottery also discovered. The artefacts will be the
subject of a larger exhibition next year, to be curated
by Mr Knight, Dig Director, and Mrs Harriett
Goodspeed, Museum Assistant.

Ruth felt a small thrill at seeing her mum's name on
the display card. She recalled their journey from Rook
Farm to London six months earlier, as Mr Knight's car
crawled through the melting snow. She'd sat half
dozing, listening to her mum and Mr Knight chatter
excitedly about the finds, exchanging views and
information as well as what seemed to be a growing
respect for one another. Six weeks later Ruth had been
surprised and delighted to find her mum had been
offered a new, paid position assisting Mr Knight on a
museum dig at the farm. While Ruth still found Mr

Knight bullish and overbearing at times, he now acknowledged her with a nod and a smile, sometimes even pausing to question her again about the day she and Joe had found the treasure in Eel Field. On these occasions she would stand tall and speak clearly, proud of all that she and her friend had achieved.

"The Rook Farm treasure was certainly a substantial discovery," Mr Knight said now, hovering at Ruth's mum's side. "It's an important addition to the British Museum's collection."

"The money we received from its sale has saved our farm," said Mary gratefully. She had completely recovered from her illness after a period of rest. "I'm also pleased I could donate some of the proceeds to our local museum and to Mrs Hartest. I think my husband and Mr Hartest would have liked that."

Joe gave his mum a proud smile and Ruth felt gratified by Mary's words. She knew from her mum's frequent visits to the farm, and from the letters she and Joe had exchanged, that the bank had been astounded by the archaeological discovery and newspaper headlines it had generated. With Mr Knight's help the bank had withdrawn the eviction notice. The sale of the treasure to the museum had paid off the loan, allowing enough money to buy new farm machinery which Joe had finally managed to persuade Mary was necessary. Gordon visited the farm often and Mary had learned to accept his help when it was needed and was thankful for it too.

On a return visit to the farm a few weeks earlier, Ruth had seen Joe putting the tractor to good use, now he was fifteen and worked on the farm full-time. Lenny had even woven a willow basket for Dash so he could accompany Joe as he drove the tractor round the farm. Joe's friend Fred had joined them for a picnic while swifts darted and screeched above their heads and the smells of summer and new growth surrounded them.

The last six months had changed all their lives in ways they could never have foreseen. The farm was not only flourishing, but Audrey and Terry had married (very quietly) a month earlier.

"Aunt Edith came to stay with us last month and said she was happy to see me settled at last. She was shocked to learn I'd lied about my family and taken the treasure, but said the important thing was that I owned up and realized my mistake," Audrey said to Ruth as she continued to look at the treasure.

"I'm glad for you, Audrey. Truly I am," Ruth replied, thinking of her own family.

Despite her mum's new job, the decision to leave the coach house had already been made. The third-floor flat Ruth and her mum had moved into was low-ceilinged and cosy, its front windows overlooking a line of London plane trees where their new house cat, Blossom, loved to sit and observe the birds as she preened herself in the sun. While her mum worked on the dig at Rook Farm, Ruth stayed with her dad. One spring evening, just as the daffodils had begun to bloom, she arrived home from school to find him painting the wall of her bedroom. It was a rural scene with huge cornflower-blue skies, light-yellow wheat fields and ditches and channels dancing with water.

"You talked about the big skies in the Fens with such fondness, I thought our new mural should be a little different," he'd said with a grin. "You can help me decide what we paint next. Perhaps a farmhouse, or some birds?"

Ruth had thought of Rook Farm and smiled. "Maybe we could paint a dog too. A black-and-white one. And a boy driving a tractor."

Ruth felt a slow rise of contentment now as she

watched Joe and Audrey laughing with her mum, the shiny museum assistant badge pinned to her mum's grey jumper glinting. There was a dot of ink on her chin and her hair was as wayward as ever. She was still obsessed with uncovering things from the past, but she was working hard to make a good future for them all too.

"You need to come and see this," Ruth said, leading everyone to a display cabinet further down the exhibit hall. She heard Audrey and Terry draw in sharp breaths as they leaned over the glass. The empress pepper pot sat proudly next to her twin, the silver gilt ibex pepper pot, which Ruth's mum had spoken of. Octavius's six identical silver ladles were also reunited and lay to one side.

"Mrs Hartest came to see this treasure a few weeks ago," said Ruth. "She told the police everything she knew about her husband's discoveries, and they didn't press charges."

"That was the right thing to do," said Joe. "Perhaps you'll be a detective and work for the police when you grow up, Ruth? You were pretty good at uncovering all of our secrets in the end."

Ruth grinned. "I don't know about that. I'm rather looking forward to doing some more excavating. Mum's taking me on her next dig and Mr Knight says I'll be a proper volunteer this time."

"Quite right too," said Audrey. "It's also right that other people will be able to enjoy looking at these ancient objects for years to come." She pressed a hand to the glass display cabinet and her bracelet clinked. Ruth saw the heart charms spelling Emma's name and smiled.

"Joe and I have a wedding present for you," said Ruth, reaching into her cardigan pocket. She pulled out a small box and passed it to Audrey.

"A present?" Audrey said in surprise.

"Go on, open it, love," urged Terry, his eyes twinkling.

Audrey pulled the lid off the box and smiled. She lifted out the small silver spoon charm and held it up. "My very own miniature ladle," she said, laughter dancing in her eyes.

"Here, let me attach it," said Ruth.

Audrey held out her wrist.

"I think Emma would have liked it," said Ruth, giving Audrey a warm smile.

Joe nodded in agreement.

"Come here," said Audrey, opening her arms wide.

Ruth and Joe exchanged a grin and stepped into Audrey's embrace. Ruth closed her eyes for a second, breathing in the smell of Rook Farm kitchen, Dash the dog and old things. But she could also smell something clean and fresh too. It could just have been soapflakes, but then again Ruth thought, if hope had a smell, it might have been that too.

Author's Note

Inspiration for *The Secret of the Treasure Keepers*

I've always been fascinated by the idea of finding treasure. When I was small, I would dig up my parents' flowerbeds with a trowel, hoping to find something interesting. But even though all I discovered were pieces of pottery, it still made me wonder why and how they had ended up buried in my back garden. I became so interested in archaeology, I even took part in a dig when I was older (we found nothing!) and studied the subject for a term at university.

The inspiration for *The Secret of the Treasure Keepers* came from one of my favourite places to visit in London: the British Museum. There are some incredible treasure hoards on display, but two in particular captured my imagination. The first is the Mildenhall Treasure, comprised of over thirty pieces of Roman silver tableware, including a giant dish which weighs a whopping eight kilograms (roughly the same weight as a chair!), which were ploughed up in 1942 in a field near Mildenhall in Suffolk, about half-an-hour's drive from my home.

As well as seeing the Mildenhall Treasure, what also captured my imagination was the story behind it. The story is too long to repeat in full, but the treasure wasn't reported for a few years as the person who discovered it couldn't bear to part with it. I found this amazing, and it provided the initial spark of an idea about Mr Hartest finding the ladles and pepper pot, then reburying them at Rook Farm to keep them safe during the war.

Another fantastic hoard at the museum is the Hoxne Hoard (pronounced "Hoxon"), also found in Suffolk in 1992. The Roman empress pepper pot, which inspired the one in the book, is on display and there are also some excellent photographs of it online on the museum's website. Why not take a look and see if it is how you imagined it in the story?

I went on to read about some other fascinating archaeological discoveries in the East of England, such as the Bronze-Age settlement at Must Farm near Peterborough in Cambridgeshire. It was found when an archaeologist noticed some wooden posts, which turned out to be around three thousand years old, sticking out of a quarry. Textiles, socketed axe heads and even pots containing the remains of meals were also discovered. All of this provided inspiration for Ruth and Joe's dig in the snowstorm at Rook Farm.

While the characters in *The Secret of the Treasure Keepers* do get excited about the value of the treasure they discover, they also learn about the importance of preserving things found buried in the ground and what they can teach us about how people lived long ago. Maybe you could ask a teacher or an adult to help you research archaeological finds made near your home, either online or at your local museum, and see what these tell you about the people who lived there.

Just as Ruth and Joe discover in the story, if you are lucky enough to discover an archaeological object in the ground yourself (please let me know if you do!), it's important to report it as this will help broaden our knowledge of history and archaeology. Today this can be done through the Portable Antiquities Scheme and you can find more information at https://finds.org.uk/.

I hope you enjoyed reading about my inspiration for the story and Ruth and Joe's adventures at Rook Farm. If it has given you a thirst for finding out more about archaeology, you might even want to think about joining The Young Archaeologists' Club for 8-16 year olds. It has over seventy local clubs throughout England, Northern Ireland, Scotland and Wales and more information can be found at https://www.yac-uk.org.

USBORNE QUICKLINKS

Would you like to see some of the treasure described in this book and find out more about Land Girls and life in the Fens after the Second World War? At Usborne Quicklinks we have provided links to websites where you can:

- See silver and gold artefacts from Roman Britain treasure troves
- Find out about a typical day in the life of a Land Girl
- Watch film footage of farmers in the 1940s
- Discover the devastation of German air raids on Norwich
- See a panoramic view of the Fens today

To visit these sites, go to usborne.com/Quicklinks and type in the keywords "treasure keepers".

Please follow the internet safety guidelines at Usborne Quicklinks. Children should be supervised online.

Acknowledgements

A book really is a team effort and I'd like to thank the following people who have helped make this one.

My fabulous agent Clare Wallace, who not only champions my stories but is a great listener and friend.

My lovely and quite brilliant editor Becky Walker, who is a huge support to me and my writing. Thanks also to the eagle-eyed Alice Moloney, and Helen Greathead for the copy-edits (still my favourite stage!).

Joanna Olney and the brilliant Usborne marketing and publicity team, and Fritha Lindqvist for promoting and publicizing this book.

Kath Millichope and Rachel Corcoran for their incredible work on the joyful cover, map and illustrations.

This book has required more research than any other and I'm very grateful to various experts for suggesting how my writing and the story could be made more authentic. Specific thanks to Richard Hobbs and Neil Wilkin, Curators at the British Museum, for responding to my many queries.

Catherine Johns, archaeologist and former Curator at the British Museum, for her perceptive thoughts on the role of women in archaeology in post-war Britain. I hope Harriett and Ruth have done your thoughts justice!

Faye Minter, Senior Archaeological Officer at Suffolk County Council, for the great Zoom chat and making me a bit star struck with tales of teaching actors how to use trowels on the Netflix film *The Dig*. It goes without saying that after all of this help, any archaeological inaccuracies in this story are entirely my own.

Thanks to my fellow authors, the book bloggers, promoters, reviewers, teachers, librarians, journalists, booksellers and the wonderful Usborne Community Partnerships team who help promote and sell my books. Your support means the world.

A final huge thank you to my lovely mum, husband Jeremy, children Jack and Ed, friends and work colleagues. You cheer me on and pick me up when the going gets tough and I'm eternally grateful for that.

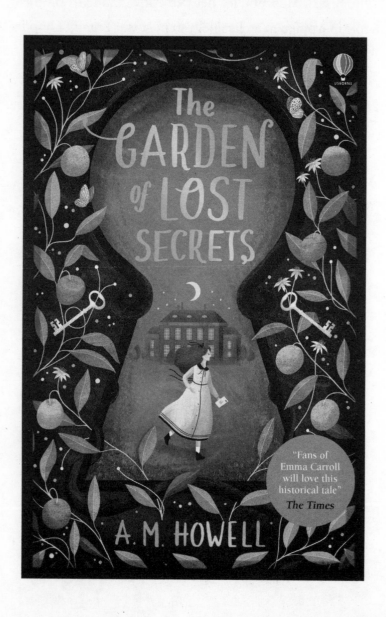

OCTOBER, 1916.

Clara has been sent to stay with her aunt and uncle while England is at war. But when she reaches their cottage on an enormous country estate, Clara is plunged into a tangle of secrets… A dark, locked room, a scheming thief, and a mysterious boy who only appears at night.

Clara has a secret of her own too – a terrible one about her brother, fighting in the war. And as the secrets turn to danger, Clara must find the courage to save herself, and those around her…

"Fans of Emma Carroll will adore this historical tale of derring-do and righted wrongs." *The Times, Children's Book of the Week*

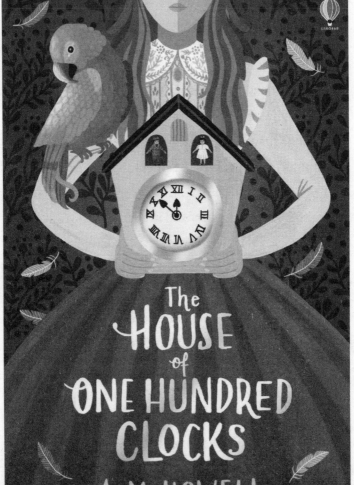

The HOUSE of ONE HUNDRED CLOCKS

A. M. HOWELL

The critically-acclaimed author of *The Garden of Lost Secrets*

JUNE, 1905.

Helena and her parrot, Orbit, are swept off to
Cambridge when her father is appointed clock-winder
to one of the wealthiest men in England. There is only
one rule: the clocks must never stop.

Soon Helena discovers the house of one hundred
clocks holds many mysteries; a ghostly figure, strange
notes and stolen winding keys… Can she work out the
house's secrets before time runs out?

**WINNER OF THE MAL PEET CHILDREN'S AWARD
WINNER OF THE EAST ANGLIAN BOOK OF
THE YEAR**

**"Howell is a hypnotically readable writer, who keeps
the pulse racing, while allowing every character
slowly to unravel."** *The Telegraph*

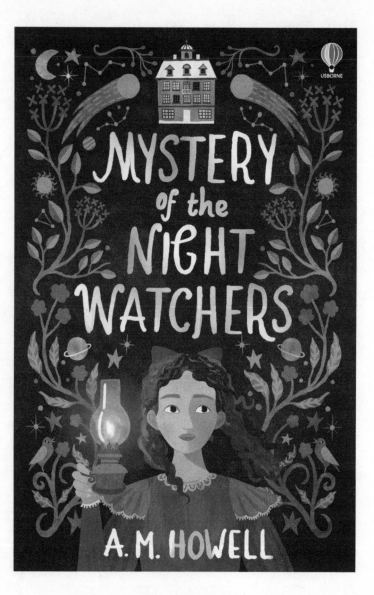